APR 06 2021

FOR JIM AND ESMOND. I HOPE THEY HAVE LIBRARIES IN HEAVEN. -JL

Blue Bronco Books
The Middle-Grade imprint of The Little Press, LLC
P.O. Box 35, Wood-Ridge N.J. 07075
www.bluebroncobooks.com

Text copyright © 2020 by Jenna Lehne
Cover art copyright © 2020 Uliana Babenko
Book design by Tobi Carter
Edited by: Crystal Branson & Michele McAvoy

Literary Consultants: Nicole Mancini, M. Ed. & Elizabeth Blye, M. Ed., M.L.I.S.

ISBN 978-0-9979580-3-4 (hardcover)
ISBN 978-0-9979580-4-1 (paperback)
ISBN 978-0-9979580-5-8 (e-book)

Our books may be purchased in bulk at a discount for promotional, educational, and business use. Please contact The Little Press sales department by email at info@littlepresspublishing.com

BONE TREE

JENNA LEHNE

Blue Bronco Books • New Jersey

CONTENTS

Chapter 1

READY, FREDDIE

THE CRACKLE OF STATIC WAKES ME UP BEFORE THE pebble against my window does.

"Echo Lima, do you read me?" Roman's voice cracks and pops over the ancient walkie-talkie that echoes from inside my nightstand—we've had matching ones since we were both seven and thought they were cool. Luckily we have them, because Mom puts my cell on lockdown every night at nine o'clock. She's old school. The call names were from when we were seven too—a spin-off from our initials. We thought they were super creative and official sounding at the time.

I sit up and scramble through my nightstand drawer until my hand wraps around the hard plastic. I turn the volume down and hold my breath, waiting for Dad's footsteps that typically shake the house. They don't come. Another pebble hits my window. My heart pumps in my chest, and I wrinkle my nose. I hold down the long plastic button on the side of the walkie. "Romeo Oxford, I'm up. Stop chucking stuff at my window."

I can hear Roman laugh without the help of the walkie-talkie. "You tryin' to chicken out on me?"

"No, but if you don't shut up, I'll get busted before I can get outa bed." I toss the walkie on my bed and stand up, still dressed in my clothes from school, so I don't have to turn on my light. I grab a can of spray butter, that's probably not even real butter, out of my nightstand—perfect for squeaky windows. The window slides up without a peep. I hop on the roof, crawl to the edge and fall into the darkness. I land in the middle of my trampoline, boom! Just as planned. I hop off and creep over the cool grass.

If I'm going to get caught, it'll happen right now. I give Mom a few seconds to turn on her bedside lamp and fling up the blinds. When she doesn't, I let out a breath and hear Roman do the same from somewhere in the shadows.

"Ready, Freddie?" He asks once I join him under the burnt-out streetlamp. The bulb went out two months ago, but no one has bothered to fix it. Mom calls the town hotline and leaves messages every other day, but they ignore her.

"I will be once you tell me where we're going." I zip up my hoodie and stuff my hands in my pockets. It's chilly even though it's September.

"You'll see." Roman grabs his bike and wheels it onto

the street. He doesn't sound the tiniest bit sleepy, even though it's way past our embarrassingly early curfews. His voice sounds stronger and even a little deeper than usual. No wonder Claire Mitchell started giving him weird looks again.

"Last time you said that we both got grounded for a week," I say.

Roman nods at the purple pegs sticking out near the back tire of his bike. "Will you just get on?" When I hop on, he sends me an evil grin. "It was so worth getting grounded, though." Roman pushes off, and we fly down the street.

I grab Roman's shoulders and smile as the wind pushes my hair out of my face. Roman was right; the last time he'd said "you'll see" had led to an epic outdoor swim with a couple of other kids in our class. We would've made it if Roman's neighbors hadn't busted us after Dustin decided to jump off the shed and into the pool.

"Is anyone else coming?" I ask as Roman turns onto an unfamiliar side street.

"Naw," he says. "I thought it could just be us tonight. I need to talk to you."

My stomach flips a little. The last time Roman needed to talk was to tell me he was breaking up with Claire Mitchell. The time before that was because his grandpa died. I think back to the last week of school, but I can't remember any new crushes or fights. He did get his English test back on Friday though, so maybe his teacher discovered he's some sort of a Shakespearean genius, and is now leaving for college immediately. This would mean I'd have to finish sixth grade alone.

"You're not leaving me for college already…are you?" I dig my fingers into his shoulders as he pops up onto the curb. I know there's a spooky forest somewhere around here, and I really hope we're not going into it.

"What are you talking about?" Roman pedals onto a grassy trail that leads us right toward the dark trees.

"Never mind," I say.

Roman skids to a halt once we reach the first, brown-leafed tree. "We have to walk from here." He leans his bike against a short, iron fence that's been there so long the trees have grown through the spaces between the metal bars.

It takes me a second to realize where we are. "You're crazy if you think I'm going in there."

Roman reaches back and puts his hand on my shoulder, "Don't be a baby, Els—"

"Shut up, Roman. You know I'm not a baby." I shove his hand away and jump the fence before he does. I'll show him who's a baby. I follow Roman down a dark, twisting path that most likely leads to the spookiest part of the Fredric Falls Cemetery. I ignore the herd of rhinos stampeding in my chest and put on my brave face. It looks kind of like my scared face only with gritted teeth.

We crunch over fallen orange leaves and hop over gnarled roots as we go farther and farther into the shadows. The cemetery smells like the fall—sweet, musty and a little bit like pumpkin. I have to look down as I walk; if I trip and rip my new jeans, Mom will know I snuck out. My heart stops pounding, but I can't shake the pebble of fear in my tummy. Too many years of whispered ghost stories have made it physically impossible to relax anywhere near dead people.

"We're here." Roman suddenly stops walking superfast, and I crash into him.

"Where's here?" I look up at the tree we're standing under. It's unlike any tree I've ever seen before, and I've been to summer camp, so I've seen every tree known to humankind. Or at least, that's what it feels like when you're stuck for two weeks at Camp Bitter Root. As I continue to stand in front of the tree, my eyes notice something odd—there's not a single piece of bark on the trunk. The trunk is smooth and so pale gray it's almost white. The branches reach for the stars, but there isn't a single leaf anywhere on them.

"It's called the Bone Tree," Roman says. "Neat, huh?"

"And creepy." I sit down on the dirt and rest my back on the tree. "So, are you gonna spill your guts or what?"

"I have to tell you the story of the Bone Tree first." Roman sits next to me and pushes his square-rimmed glasses up his nose. He got contacts for his twelfth birthday, but he wears his glasses when it's just us. He reaches into his pocket and pulls out a packet of Twinkies. He opens them and passes me one. "My brother told me about the tree last night. He came here over the weekend with his friends."

I stuff the Twinkie in my mouth, but it sits on my tongue like a brick. Snacking while scared is never a good idea. "Did you bring anything to drink?"

Roman laughs. "I didn't, sorry. Now shut up, will ya? I'm trying to tell you a ghost story."

I swallow the Twinkie hard and roll my eyes. "Go ahead, bossy pants."

Roman clears his throat like Dad does before saying grace. "Okay, once upon a time, like four hundred years ago, there was a priest named Samuel. He came over from Europe with his wife, but she died on the ship."

"How did she die?" I ask. I'm already starting to get the heebie-jeebies.

"I dunno," Roman says. "Rats or some ship disease. Rats with a weird ship disease, maybe? It doesn't matter. Anyway, Samuel settled here, in Fredric Falls, and started a church. He was happy with his congregation, but he was lonely. A month later, a huge flood wiped out a bunch of the farmland surrounding the town. A local farmer offered Samuel his only daughter, Mary, if he could plant crops on the church's land."

"He traded his daughter for dirt?" I shake my head. "What a crappy dad."

"It was a different time," Roman says. "Your dad would trade you for a herd of goats if you lived back then."

"No, he wouldn't." My dirty-blonde hair blows into my face, so I grab a handful of it and twist it into a braid.

Roman stares at my hair. "You're right. You'd be worth at least a herd...with a pig thrown in the mix."

I throw a handful of leaves at him. "What happened to Samuel and the girl? Did they get married?"

Roman nods. "They got married and fell in love. They had a little boy, and they were really happy for a couple of years. But then Mary, the wife, had an accident."

"The priest had no luck with the ladies."

Roman stands up and looks up at the glowing moon. "She was walking with her son on top of the falls right before the fall harvest."

"Oh no." I suck in my breath. Everyone in town knows you don't go near the top of the waterfall. It seems safe—the little river leading over the edge is peaceful as heck—but the rocks are smooth and slippery. One misstep and you're a goner. Waterfall soup.

"Legend has it that her son lost his little boat in the river. Mary tried to grab it, slipped and fell down the falls."

"Oh no." I feel bad for Mary. "What happened to her son?"

"Someone found him, I guess. Anyway, it's not about the son. After Mary died, Samuel, the husband, went nuts. He sent his son away and kept Mary's body locked up in his house. He prayed over her body for days—he even sent for the priests in the neighboring town—but nothing worked. Mary stayed on the table, cold and unmoving. Samuel sent the priests away and summoned an old woman...a woman who was rumored to be a witch. She performed an ancient blessing on Mary's body, full of herbs, chants and frog eyes or something. It wasn't until Mary's father showed up and, demanded the body of his daughter, that Samuel decided to lay his love to rest. He buried her in her wedding gown."

"Weird. What does any of this have to do with the tree?" I ask.

"I'm getting to that." Roman pushes his shaggy black hair out of his eyes. "The farmer dug his daughter a grave in this cemetery and planted a tree over top of her body because they couldn't afford a headstone."

I half jump, half crawl away from the tree. "Why didn't you tell me I was sitting on a dead person?"

"Because she didn't stay dead," Roman whispers.

A vicious chill crawls up my spine.

Roman keeps going. "Samuel locked himself in his house to grieve. He didn't come out until he heard reports of a woman in white roaming the cemetery."

"Creepy," I say. I crane my neck to make sure there isn't anyone in white sneaking around behind me.

Roman continues, "Yup. Anyways, Samuel spent night after night at Mary's grave, crying and begging God to show him his wife."

"Did God answer his prayers?" I try to remember my old Sunday school classes. I know people rose from the dead all the time, but I can't remember if they roamed graveyards after or not.

"Someone did, but I don't think it was God."

Chapter 2

A PEBBLE IN MY STOMACH

ROMAN WALKS IN A SLOW CIRCLE AROUND THE TREE. "On the fourth day, Samuel found his wife still dressed in her wedding gown. Samuel hugged her, but his arms went right through her. She was super weak and could barely talk. Mary told him she wasn't strong enough to stay on her own. That she needed help."

"So what did he do?" I wrap my arms around myself and hop from foot to foot. "Bring her a power bar and an energy drink?"

This earns me a full-on Roman-chuckle. For such a skinny guy, Roman has a huge laugh. "This was four hundred years ago, Els, not four. But I don't know what Samuel did to keep Mary around...we'll just have to find out."

The pebble in my stomach quickly returns. I ignore the feeling and force out a laugh. "How are we going to do that? It's probably just some dumb story Jake made up to scare you."

Like any older brother, Jake was always trying to freak out Roman and me because I was always around.

"It's true," Roman says. "It's gotta be."

"Why didn't Samuel just move on? Why would he want to stay married to a ghost?" I ask.

Roman shrugs. "I'm not sure, but if you could keep someone you loved around, wouldn't it be worth it?"

I shrug. I guess he has a point. I'd do pretty much anything to keep my parents around. Even if it meant casting spooky spells in a nightmare forest. The thought makes something in my brain snap into place. "Why are you telling me all of this?"

A sudden gust of wind pushes through the trees and swirls up, making the Bone Tree's branches dance in the moonlight.

Roman takes off his glasses and gives me a sad little smile. "Because I'm dying."

I'm instantly annoyed. "Yeah, right. Real funny, Roman." I force out a laugh because it's not a funny joke at all.

He takes a step toward me. "I'm telling the truth. Why do you think I've been excused from gym this past week?"

I shrug. "I dunno, I thought you just had a bunch of homework."

Roman shakes his head. "I'm sick…really sick."

I stare at him, waiting for him to burst out laughing and tell me this is all just one big joke. But he doesn't. Instead, his blue eyes shimmer the tiniest bit. My heart slams against my chest so hard that it actually hurts. "You're serious, aren't you?"

Roman nods.

"Okay...okay . . ." I back away from Roman.

"Wait—" Roman starts to say.

I turn and sprint down the path before he can say another word. I run as fast as I can. I don't know what else to do. The tiny pebble in my stomach is now a giant boulder, and I'm afraid if I stop running, I'll barf it up. I hop over the fence and cut through backyards, so Roman and his bike can't follow me. When I get home, I fish through the rocks surrounding Mom's flower bushes before I find the hollow one holding the house key. I burst through the front door and make it into my parent's room before I cry—though crying doesn't seem like the right word. It's more of a scream at first.

Mom is out of bed and on the ground next to me in two seconds flat. "Elsie, what's wrong?" She pulls me into her arms as she quickly examines my body making sure I'm not hurt.

"Did you have a bad dream?" Dad pulls the blanket off the bed and drapes it around Mom and me.

I shake my head and blubber, "Roman's sick, Mom. He's dying."

"Honey, it was just a dream," Mom says. She pushes my sweaty bangs off my face. "Roman is fine."

I cough and cry harder. "No, it's real life, Mom. We snuck out. I'm sorry, I'm sorry, I'm sorry. Roman is going to die. I'm sorry."

"Oh my God, Danny, get the phone." Mom rubs my back in circles like she did when I was a baby and about to throw up.

Dad calls Roman's house and talks to his mom. I can't hear much because the part in me that's supposed to turn off my tears and listen is broken.

"Okay, we'll come over tomorrow morning," Dad says before he hangs up. I hear his lips smack together, and I can tell he's mouthing words to Mom over my head.

"Do you want to sleep in here tonight?" Mom asks a few minutes later.

I nod and let Dad scoop me up.

"Y-you can't tell R-Roman I was crying." I hiccup.

"We won't." She pushes my bangs off my forehead again. "It'll be our secret."

Mom and I climb into bed. Dad puts a blanket on the floor for himself because we won't all fit in the bed. He reaches up and holds my hand really tight. They both fall asleep, but I stare out the window, wishing Mary and the Bone Tree were real and not some silly ghost story.

Chapter 3

I PROMISE

THE NEXT MORNING ROMAN'S MOM, MRS. PIERCE, PUTS A big platter of pancakes on her kitchen table. She's petite with a bit of a mom-muffin-top and has long brown hair that she always puts in a ponytail. Mr. Pierce sits next to Roman and hands him a dish stacked with pancakes. He's tall—a few feet taller than Mrs. Pierce—with hair just as dark as Roman's. Roman's big brother, Jake, doesn't eat with us. I sit across from Roman and push sliced strawberries around a pool of syrup. Our parents trade words like "leukemia" and "stage four," but all I hear is that my best friend is dying, and there's nothing I can do about it.

Once we're done eating, I follow Roman up to his room. He hasn't said much since I got there. He hasn't said anything at all, actually. He's probably mad at me for leaving him in the graveyard; he never talks when he's mad. When

Jake opened Roman's limited-edition Venom figurine, Roman didn't speak for three days. I flop down on Roman's bed and stare up at the ceiling. It still has the glow-in-the-dark stars we stuck up there back when Roman wanted to be an astronaut. I wonder what he wants to be now that he may not get to grow up.

Roman sits on the window seat covered with laundry and stares out the window. "I'm sorry," he whispers to the glass.

I shrug and blink back tears. How can I still have tears left in my body? "It's not your fault."

"It kinda is." Roman gives me a half-smile. "The doc told me to lay off the cigarettes years ago."

Only Roman would joke at a time like this. I blink a few more times and sit up. His room looks the same. The walls are still dark blue, and books and clothes still cover the floor. The tall, narrow bookshelf is still cluttered with toys; I mean "collectibles." Once, I called them "toys," and he had a baby-flip. Roman doesn't look sick either. Sure, he's a little pale, but he's always been pretty white. His clothes still fit—if anything, they look a little tight around the shoulders. His blue eyes are bright and focused, not sick looking.

"So… what's leukemia?" I smooth the wrinkles out of his gray quilt.

Roman joins me on his bed. "It's cancer."

"Oh…" I say, unable to speak any more words. I knew cancer was bad—my aunt had it.

"Yeah, it's uh…pretty advanced." Roman picks a loose string off of his sleeve. "I'm starting chemo this week and everything."

I look down at the ground and let my hair fall into my face. "What does chemo do to you? My aunt had it, but I guess I don't know what it does to your body."

"They put these cancer-killing chemicals right into my blood. The medicine will attack the cancer cells and hopefully fix me all up." Roman rattles off the information as if he's reading it straight out of a boring brochure.

"Will it hurt?"

"The doctor said it will make me sick and pretty tired, but that just means it's working." Roman bumps his shoulder into mine.

"Is there a chance the medicine, the chemo or whatever, will get all of the cancer, and you'll be okay?" I drag my eyes up and look Roman right in the eye. "And don't you dare lie to me."

Roman gives me a funny little smile. "There's always a chance."

"Okay, good." I let out a long, deep breath. "I don't want to sound like a jerk, but you don't seem that sick."

"I didn't even feel that bad until a few days ago," Roman says. "I've been tired for a while, but I thought that was just because I've been staying up late, binging on Netflix and stuff. But then my joints started hurting. My mom thought it was just growing pains. She didn't take me to the hospital until I started getting these."

Roman lifts up his shirt, showing me apple-sized bruises along his ribs. "I started to bruise like I was in ninja training, and we figured out something was wrong."

The purple stains covering his skin are too much for me to handle. I squeeze my eyes shut and lean back against the wall.

"Do you…um…want a hug?" Roman asks. "They seem to make my parents feel better."

"Whatever, I don't care." My voice does this stupid cracking thing. My throat burns from the trillion tears I'm holding back.

Roman inches closer.

I lean forward, grabbing handfuls of Roman's Ninja Turtle T-shirt and shove my face into his neck. I try not to cry, but I can't help it. In seconds I'm bawling like a baby.

Roman wraps his arms around my shoulders and rests his chin on my head. "It's going to be okay, Els, you'll see."

He sounds so strong I almost believe him.

"Please don't leave me," I sob against his throat, my tears soaking the front of his shirt.

"I won't leave, I promise." Roman squeezes me even closer. "I promise."

Chapter 4

HALL OF KNOWLEDGE

ROMAN'S PARENTS PULL HIM OUT OF SCHOOL AFTER HIS second round of chemo.

"This is so stupid." Roman stuffs binders and gym clothes into a bright green duffle bag his parents made him bring since all his stuff wouldn't fit in his backpack. "I feel fine. Don't I look fine?"

I give Roman a long look. His face is a little puffy from the steroids the doctors gave him, but you can only tell if you look really close. His lips are chapped and cracked in lots of places, but at least the sores are gone. He wouldn't leave the house when he had mouth sores, even though his doctor told him it was a totally normal side effect from the treatment.

"Well, you're kinda pale, and your hair is a little greasy. Other than that, you look fine." I pretend I don't notice him struggling to lift the duffle bag onto his shoulder—especially since he is already carrying his backpack on his back. I start to tell him how bummed I'll be without him here, but I stop myself. Roman needs to worry about getting better, not about me having a few lame weeks without my best friend. Besides, I'll still see him after school.

"Thanks." Roman sighs as he drags his fingertips of his free hand along the lockers as though he's saying goodbye to the worn metal.

We walk down the empty hallway toward the parking lot. Roman waited to pack up his stuff until everyone left for the day, even Mr. Wilson's detention class.

I couldn't believe it when he walkied me the night before. "But don't you wanna… I dunno… say goodbye to everyone?" I asked him.

"Why? So my teachers can pat my head and tell me how sorry they are?" Roman snorted.

I guess he had a point; having one last day of anything seems like a bad omen.

At the last minute, Roman turns and goes back up the stairs instead of going out to the parking lot.

"Where are you going?" I follow him and grab the handles of the duffle bag, so he doesn't have to carry it anymore.

"I forgot. I need to grab a book from the library first." Roman coughs when we reach the top of the stairs, his breath growing heavy, but he keeps on walking into the dimly lit library.

"Why? Your parents will buy you whatever you want," I say. Since Roman got sick, his parents do whatever Roman wants. If he wants pizza, he gets pizza. If he wants to watch a certain show, they all watch it. He's not taking advantage of it too much, even though a lot of kids I know probably would.

"I can't get this book off of the internet." Roman drops his backpack near the front desk.

Ms. Young, the ancient librarian, is perched behind her desk sorting books. She looks up as we tiptoe past her, but she doesn't say anything, only smiles a little as we disappear into the bookstacks.

We wander down the rows of books, going deeper and deeper into the "Hall of Knowledge," as Ms. Young calls it. However, you rarely saw someone actually checking out a book, especially since laptops were donated to the library. I stop in front of a random shelf and pick up an old, thin book and open it. The pages are dark as though someone spilled tea on them, and the smell reminds me of Ms. Young.

The fluorescent lights flicker overhead as one of the glowing tubes dies. Roman turns around and scans the shelves behind me— his eyes narrowing as he looks for a specific book. I return the weathered book to the shelf and walk further down the aisle, trailing my fingers along the cracked and wrinkled spines.

Roman finds his book and carries it up to the desk. I follow behind him, the book leaving a trail of dust and bits of paper.

"Ms. Young, I was wondering if I could take this home?" Roman had grabbed a monster of a book off the shelf. I mean, it's enormous.

Ms. Young peers at Roman over her wire-rimmed glasses. "Reference books are for library use only."

"Can I just borrow it for a couple of days? I promise I'll be careful," Roman says.

"If I let one student take one of those books out, I'll have to let them all take one, and suddenly we'll have mayhem." Ms. Young overestimates kids' enthusiasm for reference books.

"He's sick," I say, finally finding my voice. "He's being homeschooled until he gets better, so he can't come to the library and read it."

Ms. Young slides her wire-rimmed glasses down her tiny, pointed nose and stares at Roman for a long minute. Her voice creaks when she finally speaks, sounding more like a wooden door opening than a person. "If I see one pizza stain or torn page, I will make you dust shelves until you graduate."

After Ms. Young scans the book and his library card, Roman slides the book into his backpack. "Yes ma'am."

Before Roman can get to it, I hoist the duffle bag back onto my shoulder, I refuse to let him carry both. His hair is starting to stick to his forehead, and his breathing is heavy again.

"You okay?" I ask.

"Yup."

I roll my eyes. "Tell me the truth."

Roman grunts and nods. His code for "leave it alone, Els."

We finally leave the school out the side door and run directly into Roman's mom.

"I was getting worried about you two." Mrs. Pierce pushes Roman's hair off his forehead. "You're burning up, sweetheart."

"I'm fine." Roman lets her fuss over him a little and puts up with her checking his temperature every three steps. When she tries to buckle his seat belt for him, he finally snaps. "Mom, seriously!"

He looks instantly ashamed. "Sorry," he mumbles, but I know he's not talking about the seat belt.

Neither is Mrs. Pierce. "Nothing to apologize for."

She turns away and swipes a hand over her face. She looks as though she's crying, but by the time she pops into the driver's seat, she's all smiles.

Mrs. Pierce babbles about white blood cell counts as if I have the slightest clue what she's talking about. I dig around in the duffle bag and find Roman's favorite Thor Pen. I grab the pen and write *research white blood cells* on my palm. Mrs. Pierce ends her tirade with, "So that's what I learned from the Internet today. It really is a wealth of information. Elsie, dear, am I taking you home?"

Roman answers for me. "She's staying for supper, and then we're doing homework. My teachers said it's really important I keep up with all of my classes, so I'm not behind when I go back."

She grips the steering wheel a little tighter. "That's a great idea. I hope you're both hungry because I've been slow cooking a ham all day." Since Roman's been sick, his mom has been missing a lot of work and slow cooking every kind of meat imaginable. Today it's ham.

Roman's dad arrives home from work just as we pull into the driveway. He grabs the duffle bag and backpack before I can and carries them both inside. I run up to Roman's room while he stays downstairs to give his dad a play-by-play of his day.

"Roman? Did you play Assassin's Creed on my account?" Roman's brother, Jake, asks as he walks into Roman's room.

Oh great. I never know what to say to Jake. When we were kids, it was totally fine; Jake would hang out with us all the time. But when he started eighth grade, he turned into one of the cool kids and totally stopped hanging out with Roman whenever I was over. Now he pretty much pretends I don't exist, so instead of looking up at Jake, I pick a spot on the floor and stare at it.

"Oh," he says when he sees me, all traces of annoyance flowing out of him until he's left bored and uninterested. "It's you."

Jake doesn't say anything else until I peek back up at him. Sometimes I can't believe Roman and Jake are related. Roman is fair skinned with dark hair and blue eyes, whereas Jake is blonde, like me, with tanned skin and pale green eyes the color of mint chocolate chip ice cream. Roman is built like a willow tree, and Jake is more like a strong maple— like I said, I've seen a lot of trees. The only thing they have in common is their towering height. Jake shot up to six feet on his thirteenth birthday, and Roman is already almost five foot six, and we're only in sixth grade.

I wait for Jake to tease me or worse, pretend I'm not even there, but he doesn't. Instead, he sits on the bed. His eyes drop to the floor. "How's my little brother doing?"

"Uh, he's good. He's kinda bummed your parents yanked him out of school, but he's feeling ok." I don't add "today" at the end of the sentence even though I'm thinking it.

Jake does it for me. "So he's better than he was on Wednesday?"

I wrinkle my nose remembering the gross details. "Much better. Roman made sure to tell me all about it."

Roman was so sick, a few days after his Monday chemo, he couldn't even get out of bed to puke. I wasn't allowed over that day, but he filled me in on all the grody details.

"You should have seen it. There was puke everywhere. And I mean everywhere. It was all down the hallway, in the bathroom, and in my parent's room." Roman always made sure to fill me in on any embarrassing stories that happened to him because of the chemo.

I quickly recap to Jake what Roman told me, hoping to ease the awkward tension in the room. We both chuckle even though nothing was truly funny, and Jake already knew the story.

"I'm happy my killer disease is so funny to you guys," Roman says from the doorway.

We crack up again, but this time Roman laughs too. I guess we all have pent up emotions. On his way out, Jake bumps my shoulder with his fist. He doesn't say anything and leaves.

Roman shuts the door behind him and crawls onto the bed with the big book. "So what's in this thing anyway?"

I lean over and try to read the tiny writing on the page Roman flipped to. A blurry photo stares up at me, dark hair with blue eyes, a stern but kinda handsome face. The name *Samuel* is scrawled underneath.

"It's all of the town's old archives. You can find most of this stuff online, but the interesting stories always seem to get left out."

"Are you looking for a certain story?"

"Yup." Roman flips through a few more pages. "I'm looking for anything and everything on Samuel, Mary and the Bone Tree."

"Why are you so obsessed with the Bone Tree?" I ask.

A flicker of guilt stabs me in the heart. Maybe I shouldn't be so honest with Roman, but I don't want him to get his hopes up that some legend about a tree could help him. Besides, Roman doesn't need the tree. The chemo is going to work, and he's going to live until he's old enough for fake teeth and hard candies.

"All stories come from a little bit of truth," Roman says.

"Are you sure you don't want to…I don't know…do some important things? Like try to download the new Aquaman or, better yet, ask Make a Wish to let you meet Aquaman?" I try to read the book upside down.

"Researching the Bone Tree is the most important thing." Roman flashes me his trademarked troublemaker grin—only this one is a little different. He looks scared, maybe even a little desperate. "How else are you going to bring me back?"

Chapter 5

20 PERCENT CHANCE

"YOU WANT ME TO DO WHAT NOW?" I TRY TO STAND UP, but my feet get tangled in Roman's blanket. A lump the size of a baseball lodges in my throat.

"You heard me." Roman flips a page and looks at me. "When I die, I want you to use the Bone Tree to bring me back."

"But the tree is just a legend," I say.

"There's something about it that we're missing. Samuel didn't just bury Mary under that tree—remember the end of the story? Mary said that she needed help to stay around. We'll research the crap out of this thing, Els. We'll find out what made Mary be able to stay with Samuel." Roman shrugs. "If it doesn't work, I don't think I'll be able to get any deader."

I groan and flop onto my back. My face is dangerously close to Roman's feet, but at least he's wearing socks. I squeeze the tip of my nose. "Can you be serious for one second?" I squeak, holding my nostrils tighter.

Roman spins around and lies down, so his head is next to mine. I can smell the cinnamon gum in his mouth, and the fabric softener his mom uses. The combination smells safe, just like Roman. Not like the new smell of bleach and ammonia that he's been smelling like. *What am I going to do if I lose that smell?*

"I've never been more serious about anything, Els." Roman pushes his glasses up his nose. "My parents and doctor are being super positive, but there's still a chance. . ."

Roman's words stutter out in chunks.

"Th-there's s-still . . a chance . . th-that I'll die..."

"You don't know that for sure," I say as the baseball lump triples in size.

"I Googled it," Roman says matter-of-factly. "Even if everything goes absolutely perfect, there's still at least a 20 percent chance I'm going to die. I know there's only a 1 percent chance that the legend is real, but why wouldn't I try to lower my chance of dying by that 1 percent?"

I cross my arms. "You're not using the Bone Tree as a reason to give up, right? You still have to fight and try your total hardest not to die, Roman. This is Plan B—the backup plan."

"Yup, the Bone Tree is our last resort." Roman holds up his pinky, and I grab onto it with my own. "It's not going to be so bad, Els. It's not like you need to do a spell or kill a cat. You just need to help me research—for now."

"Okay, I'll do it," I say. Roman's confidence makes the lump disappear. "Where do we start?"

—

That night Dad lets me take the laptop to bed—something usually allowed only for study sessions and weekends—and I Google the crap out of *Fredric Falls, Bone Tree and The Woman in White*.

There are a few urban legend websites that confirm Roman's story about a woman in white roaming the cemetery, but there aren't any pictures or solid proof. I close the computer and grab my teddy bear.

"Well, Mr. Bear," I say to his soft, worn face. "It looks like we're going to have to find her ourselves."

—

Roman and I meet up every afternoon for the next two weeks, except for the days he has doctor appointments or treatment. On those days, he walkies me when he goes to bed. At first, I wouldn't hear from him until then, but it's getting earlier and earlier every day.

I'm finishing up my English homework, just after eight, when my walkie crackles to life.

"Echo, Li—" Roman starts to cough.

I wait for him to finish hacking up a lung. "What's up?"

"Not much," Roman says weakly. "Do you have an update for me?"

I dig a folded piece of paper out of my backpack and open it up. "Sure do, I found out that Samuel and Mary's last name is Simon from another big old dusty book. I traced Samuel's family tree all the way down to his great-great-great-grandson. He used to live here, but he died a few years ago."

"The whole family stayed in Fredric Falls?" Roman's voice perks up.

"Yup," I say. "I found Samuel's address too. He used to be the caretaker of the graveyard."

"You found all that out in one day?" Roman asks.

"It was easy," I admit. "Ms. Young is making us do research on our ancestors. We all got access to an ancestry website. So, instead of plugging in my family info, I plugged in *Samuel Simon* and voila!"

"Pretty awesome," Roman says.

"Wanna hear something kinda neat?" I ask. "My dad is actually Samuel Simon's great, great, great…a lot of greats, nephew! Isn't that weird?"

"So weird," Roman agrees.

"Now what do we do?"

"I think we need to do some field research," Roman says. "We should go back to the Bone Tree and see if we find anything weird out there."

"Other than dead bodies, right?" I shake off a shiver. I'm not usually this much of a wimp.

"Right." Roman coughs again. "Wanna go tomorrow night? I'm feeling kind of crappy, so there's no way my mom will let me leave the house now."

"It's okay, I'll be ready to go whenever you walkie me tomorrow. Night, Roman."

"Roger that," Roman croaks. "Night, Els..."

I put the walkie on my nightstand and pray for the millionth time that Roman will get better.

—

Tomorrow is a half-day at school, so I don't have to spend too long answering questions about Roman. Claire is by far the worst; she's ignored me forever, but since Roman left, I'm like her new bestie.

"Hi Elsie," she says when I stop at my locker at the end of the day. "How's our Roman?"

I hate it when she calls him "our" Roman. He isn't hers. I stuff my binder in my locker and grab my backpack. "He's good."

"That's so great." Claire beams at me. "My mom is calling his mom this weekend. We made a bunch of soup, so we're going to bring it to him. I'm sure it'll make him feel better."

The muscles holding up my fake smile fail on me, and I slam my locker shut. "He doesn't have a cold, Claire. He has cancer. Soup isn't going to 'make him feel better.'"

Claire gasps and her sparkly green eyes fill with tears. Mine do too, but only because I've never said the word *cancer* out loud before. The word "cancer" now grows legs and dropkicks me in the stomach. For a second, I can't breathe. Claire runs away, blubbering into her pink cell phone. I clutch my stomach and suck in gulps of stinky school air.

I squeeze my eyes shut and smack my palm into my forehead. *Why am I such a jerk?* I know soup will make Roman feel better—he loves soup—and Claire is just trying to help. I should run after her and apologize, but I don't think I can do it without crying. And I'm not letting Claire, or anyone, see me cry.

Mom is waiting for me outside. "What's wrong?"

"Nothing." I climb in the car and buckle up.

"Elsie, you need to talk to us about this whole Roman thing." She reaches over and grabs my hand.

"There's nothing to talk about." I yank my hand away and stare out the window. I try to swallow around the baseball lump that still seems to be in my throat.

"Well, I'm here if you change your mind. Your dad and I love you so much, kid."

Mom's hands flutter around as though she's thinking about holding my hand, again. She must have decided against it because she grabs the steering wheel instead.

"Love you back," I murmur.

We drive home in silence. I do my homework in my room, only coming out to say goodnight. I try watching a movie on Dad's ancient laptop, but nothing can dislodge this weight dangling from my heart. I feel like there's a storm cloud over my head, just waiting to destroy my world. The only thing that keeps my brain busy is organizing, which is so unlike me. I can't even keep my locker clean, and it's only two feet wide. I push my double bed into the corner of my room, dig out my winter comforter and put it on my bed. I chuck the other blankets in the laundry and fall facedown onto my pillow. At some point, I fall asleep, but it isn't a good sleep. It's full of nightmares where everything is normal except Roman is dead, and the Bone Tree doesn't work.

—

Roman doesn't wake me up until ten at night. I listen to him recite my name over the walkie, and then he waits while I say his code name back.

"Sorry I took so long," he says. "My parents have turned every night into some kind of family event. Tonight we watched *Harry Potter and the Prisoner of Azkaban*. I fell asleep before Harry rode the hippogriff. Then I had to fake falling asleep once I went to bed too."

I know he probably wasn't faking it. He probably passed out again, but I don't say anything.

"That's okay. I had tons of homework, anyway. I'll be right down." I stash the walkie and open the window and stick one leg out just as my door opens.

"Where do you think you're going?" Dad pushes his glasses off his face and rubs the stubble on his cheeks. His dark blonde hair is starting to get a little gray around his ears. Mom says it's from stress.

"Um, to the library," I say lamely. I'm so busted.

Dad sits on my bed. "Is Roman outside waiting for you?"

I look out the window. "Yeah."

Dad stands up. "Okay."

"I can go?" I ask in disbelief.

"Yes, but don't tell your mom." Dad walks back out into the hallway. "And use the door like a regular person. You're going to break your neck on that trampoline."

"Thank you, thank you, thank you." I hug Dad on my way out through the door and not the window this time.

He gives me the same sad smile everyone else gives me. "Have fun."

Chapter 6

WE HAVE TO TRY

"YOUR DAD CAUGHT YOU SNEAKING OUT, AND HE STILL let you leave?" Roman puffs as he pedals up the tiny hill leading to the cemetery.

"Yup." I grab Roman's shoulders a little tighter. He turns the bike onto the grass.

"You should've let me pedal." I climb off and wait for Roman to do the same.

"I'm fine, Els." He gets off the bike and leans it against a short, little tree. He shrugs off his backpack and lobs it over the black fence. "Let's get this over with. I'm kinda tired, but it's not from pedaling. The meds the doc gave me suck all the energy out of me."

I hop over the fence and heave the pack onto my shoulder. I trip twice before Roman catches up to me and shines the light down the path. When I trip again, Roman takes my hand to help me up. His skin is cold and dry, not clammy like I thought it'd be. We make it to the Bone Tree a few minutes later. Each branch rustle and leaf crinkle send a chill up my spine. I zip my sweatshirt up and kneel next to Roman. It's cold out, but there isn't a cloud in the sky. The moon is bright enough that we can see without flashlights.

"I have a question," I say. "How am I supposed to get you here in the first place? I can't make your parents bury you under the tree."

Roman falls back onto his butt. He reaches into his pocket and pulls out the red metal Swiss Army knife that Jake got him for Christmas last year. "Do you have a bag or anything?"

I pat my jacket pocket and nod. "I brought snacks." I dig the bag of cookies out of my pocket and empty the cookies directly into my mouth. I shake the baggie upside down to get rid of the crumbs and pass it to Roman.

"Thanks." Roman shakes his head at the sight of my cheeks full like a chipmunk's. He twists a big chunk of his black hair around his finger and pulls it tight. He cuts the hair off with a flick of the Swiss Army knife and puts the hair in the cookie bag.

"Do you think that'll work as good as burying you?" I ask. "I mean, Mary's entire body is under the tree, not just some of her hair."

Roman taps the skinny blade against his chin. "Maybe. This should help."

Before I can stop him, Roman drags the knife over his thumb. Blood wells up from the cut and Roman lets it drip over the hair.

"There you go," he says. "If the Bone Tree doesn't work, freeze this and clone me in fifty years."

"Gross." I wrinkle my nose and take the baggie. I quadruple check it's sealed shut before I put it back in my pocket.

Cracking twigs and low voices fill the air. "Someone's coming," I say. I grab Roman's sleeve and tug him backward until we're hidden in the shadows of the trees.

Branches snap in the distance, but they're growing closer. A low wail drifts on the cool breeze, making my entire body explode with goose bumps. I reach for Roman's hand and squeeze it as hard as I can. A beetle scurries over our fingers and something slithers near my head, but I don't budge. The trees surrounding another path start to quiver and shake. It's the Woman in White. It has to be.

"Get ready to run," I whisper into Roman's ear.

"Mona, honey, this is insane," a deep voice says from one of the cemetery's many trails.

I let out a tiny sigh. "It's not a ghost."

"We have to try," a lady says. Her voice is shaking as though she's trying not to cry. "You promised we'd try."

"I don't think this is a good idea," he says. "It's just going to upset you even more."

The man steps into the moonlight. He appears to be at least thirty, and he's holding a lady's hand. The woman looks the same age, but her big, wet eyes make her look younger.

She's holding a small teddy bear. They move toward the Bone Tree slowly as though they're waiting for something to pop out from behind it.

"The stories are true," the woman says. "I don't know why you don't believe me."

The man runs his hand over his face, but he doesn't say anything.

The woman continues, "The story says that the priest buried his wife under this tree, and she came back. Maybe if we bury something of Theo's, he'll come back too, even if it's just for a minute. We have to try. Please, Kevin. We need to try." She falls to her knees and claws at the dirt with her hands. Her husband helps her and soon they have a small, deep hole. Together, they lower the teddy bear into the ground. The man covers the hole and stands up. He looks around hopeful, but as the seconds go by, his face falls.

"Why isn't it working?" Mona asks.

Kevin sighs. "I don't know, honey."

Mona starts to cry. "It's supposed to work. We're supposed to see him. That's what the legend said. Where is Theo?"

Kevin shakes his head and mutters a swear word under his breath.

"Oh, I forgot," Mona says smiling desperately. "The stories say you have to bury something else too—a token from someone else who has died. Give me your dad's watch. We'll bury it next to Theo's bear, and your dad's watch will give Theo energy. That's what the priest did…each time his wife grew weak, he brought her back with a locket or a letter of someone who had died."

I look at Roman and give him my *What is she talking about* look.

Kevin reaches into his pocket and pulls out a handkerchief. "Try this, honey. It was my uncle's."

Mona snatches it and plunges it into the ground.

Again Roman and I wait with wide eyes—and again, nothing happens.

Mona throws herself to the ground and beats the earth with her fists.

"It's okay." Kevin shushes her. He scoops her up and carries her like a baby toward the path they came from. "It's going to be okay."

Roman and I don't say anything until they disappear. We come out of the bushes and step back out into the moonlight.

"The Bone Tree didn't work for them," I say numbly. Roman is going to die, and I'm never going to see him again.

"Maybe it only works if they do it our way. They didn't bury any part of Theo." Roman points to the baggie in my pocket. "Don't give up on me yet, Els."

"I won't," I say fiercely. I march up to the Bone Tree and drop to my knees. "Did you hear what they said about other dead people's stuff? That it's the missing piece of the puzzle…that's what Samuel did to keep Mary around."

Roman grins. "I guess you're going to have to start reading the obituaries."

I don't pretend to laugh at his joke. I glance at the tree. "Want to see if we can find any more stuff buried? Just to see if the story is true?"

"What do you think?" Roman asks as he crouches behind me and plunges his hands into the dirt.

Chapter 7

PEARL EARRINGS

I SCRATCH AT THE TIGHTLY PACKED DIRT AS IF IT'S A contest. If Roman's life clock is running out of time, I'm not going to waste a single second. I rake out handfuls of dirt until my fingers drag against something metal.

"I think I found something," I say.

Roman clambers over and sticks his nose in the hole. "What's that?"

I bump him with my shoulder. "Get your face outa there and let me find out." I reach into the hole and dig around the mystery object. My fingers brush against, what feels like, a small, square box.

"Pull it out." Roman wipes his forehead with the back of his hand.

I shove my fingers farther into the dirt and wrap my hand around the box. As I pull it out, an icy breeze washes over me. It's so strong that my hair whips our faces, making me scream and drop the box onto the ground. I zip my sweat-shirt all the way up to my chin, as far as it will go. "What was that?"

"I don't know." Roman shivers beside me.

"This is getting creepy." I turn the tin over; it's weathered and painted red and white.

"Can I see that?" Roman holds out his hand.

I pass him the faded red and white box. "I think there's something in it."

Roman opens it and dumps the contents out into his palm. Two pearl earrings fall out just as a low, sad moan fills the air.

"Coyotes?" I pull my hood onto my head. There's something about having my head covered that makes me feel a little bit safer. Like when you were a kid, and you hid under your blankets in bed if you thought a monster was in your bed-room. Like, if there was actually a monster in your bedroom, the blanket over your head would somehow protect you. Silly.

"That doesn't sound like any coyote I've ever heard." Roman pockets the earrings, drops the tin back into the hole and stands up. He helps me up and pushes me back-ward, so I'm sandwiched between him and the tree.

The moan turns into a wail—the kind people make when someone dies. The cry makes my stomach feel like it's being stabbed with an icicle. The air gets chilly, and all I can smell is the loose dirt.

The scream sounds again. *Will I sound like that if Roman dies?*

The sound swirls around us just like the cold air did. I grab handfuls of Roman's jacket and bury my face between his bony shoulder blades. "Make it stop, Roman."

The scream gets so loud that suddenly Roman and I are thrown off of our feet. I tumble into the dirt and Roman lands in a pile of old branches. The screaming gets louder until I have to grab the sides of my head to keep it from throbbing.

And then it's quiet. Too quiet.

A column of fog swirls around the trunk of the tree until it starts to twist into the shape of a woman.

"It's her." I gasp. "It's the Woman in White!"

"Run!" Roman yells. He jumps up, pulls me to my feet and we run faster than we've ever run before.

We duck under branches and jump over rocks, but I'm not fast enough. The Woman in White—Mary—stops me before I can reach the fence. Her gnarled fingers snare my hair and drag me back. I scream and reach for her hands behind me, but I can't feel anything. This is it—the ghost has caught me. She's going to kill me or make me her slave forever.

"Roman! Help!" Tears shoot out of my eyes and cover my cheeks.

Roman flies onto the path and covers my mouth with his hand. "It's just a branch, Els. It's okay." He untangles my hair from the branches.

"Thanks." I look up at him. He's so pale his skin looks gray. The skin underneath his eyes looks purple and bruised. I need to get him home. Now.

"No problem," he says weakly. He pats his pocket, and the earrings jingle in the tin. "We better go."

Roman doesn't argue when I climb onto the bike seat. He steps onto the pegs—he put on especially for me—and grabs my shoulders.

I pedal as hard and as fast as I can, and I don't stop until I get to Roman's house. "Wait," he says when I put my feet on the ground. "I need to take you home."

"I can walk," I say. "Are you okay?"

"You're not walking home alone, Els. I'll crawl if I got to," Roman says as he stumbles up the sidewalk.

I grab him before he face-plants into the flower bed. "Okay fine, but we're going inside to take a break first."

We sneak around the house and into the backyard. The TV is on in the rec room, but we don't have any other way inside. Roman isn't strong enough to climb the lattice—his usual method for sneaking in and out. I peek in the window and find Jake sprawled out on the couch, fast asleep.

"We're all good," I whisper. I throw Roman's arm around my shoulder and open the back door.

Roman makes it two feet inside before his eyes roll back in his head, and he drops like a bag of bricks.

I yelp and tap Roman's cheeks. "Wake up, Rom."

His eyes open a little before they flicker shut again. I grit my teeth and pull him into a sitting position. "Please wake up. We're home, Roman."

Suddenly, a lamp flicks on.

"Roman?" Jake rubs the sleep out of his eyes. When he sees Roman, he jumps off the couch and runs over to us. "What happened to him?"

"He's okay, he's just tired." I push Roman's damp hair off his forehead. His skin is burning hot. I snatch my hand away. "What do we do?"

Footsteps thud down the hallway above us. "Roman, where are you?" His dad's deep voice echoes down the stairs.

Jake springs to his feet and pulls Roman's jacket and shoes off and chucks them behind the entertainment center. "Go hide outside. I'll come out as soon as I can."

I run out the door and hide behind the huge oak tree I broke my wrist climbing last summer. I spy through the window as Roman's parents run into the rec room. I can't hear anything, but Mrs. Pierce looks like she's screaming at Jake. A few minutes later, every light in the house is on.

He's going to be okay. I lean against the tree and close my eyes. I whisper the same prayer my Nanny does whenever she sees a sick person, and it makes me feel a little better. Roman is going to be all right.

I sneak out of the backyard and run home as fast as I can, cutting through a churchyard just in case Mary is on my tail.

Chapter 8

BRING YOU BACK

CANCER MOVIES SUCK. FOR STARTERS, THE MAIN characters aren't convincing at all. Usually they look like someone dusted their face with chalk before spritzing their face with water. If you get a good actress, she may even cough up apple juice into a garbage can. For some reason, the movies don't show the sick kid's sheets being stripped after he wet his bed during his fifth nap of the day. They skip over the part where the sick kid hurls on his best friend too.

"I'm so sorry, Els," Roman groans from his seat on the edge of the tub. The corner of his mouth still has toothpaste on it.

"It's no big deal." I try not to gag. I dunk my head in the sink and wash chunks of puke out of my hair. I'm wearing Roman's superman T-shirt while his mom washes mine. I wring my hair out and wrap it in a towel.

"Do you wanna go downstairs and watch a movie?" Roman asks. He's supposed to be on bed rest, but his favorite sheets are still in the dryer.

"Sure," I say. "Can I pick?"

"Nope." Roman goes down the stairs, shaky at first, but he steadies up before we reach the main floor. "There's got to be some perks to being sick."

"Roman!" Mrs. Pierce shouts. "Time for your meds."

"I'm right here, Mom." Roman leans on the kitchen island and holds out his hand.

"Where are you going?" She unscrews six containers and pulls out a pill from each. "Your doctor said you're supposed to rest, so the disease doesn't get any worse."

"We're just going to the rec room." Roman swallows the handful of pills—two at a time with a glass of water. His meds have doubled since our trip to the Bone Tree. Sneaking out made everything worse.

"Make sure you cover-up. It's kind of chilly down there." She smiles at me and my towel-covered head. "I'll let you know when your shirt's clean."

I smile back. "Thanks, Mrs. P." Since I've been around for like, ever, Mrs. Pierce told me I could shorten her name to Mrs. P. I do what I'm told.

The big book is sitting on the couch downstairs. Roman must've read that thing a million times already—I don't know why it's still kicking around.

"I feel like we're missing a part of the story," Roman says once he's settled. "What did burying tokens do to help Mary? I know the story says she needed help to stay around—what help did the tokens give her?"

I shrug.

"I've read this stupid book back to front, but it doesn't say anything on what happened to Mary. Neither does the entire freaking internet," Roman says. "I'm running out of time, and I can't find the answer."

Roman chucks the book on the floor and crosses his arms, blinking furiously.

Oh, Roman.

It hurts my heart to see him so mad, but if I try to talk to him about it now, he's going to clam up. I climb off the couch and grab the book. "Ms. Young would kill you if she saw you chuck it like that."

Roman laughs a little. "Promise you won't rat me out?"

"I promise." I set the book next to me. Something shuffles a little. "Oh crap, I think some of the pages are loose."

"Pass it here," Roman says.

I hand him the book.

He holds it up to his head and shakes it gently. He turns it over in his hands until he's holding it upside down. "I think there's something inside the cover."

I scramble over. "Seriously?"

"Yeah, look!" Roman points to a fine line of black stitching along the bottom of the tattered, leather cover. "One second."

Roman digs in his pocket and pulls out his Swiss Army

knife. He flips open a small blade and runs it along the stitched seam of the cover. The old thread pops open.

"Mrs. Young is really going to kill you now," I say, my heart is now beating as fast as a hummingbird's. "Flip it upside down," I whisper.

He flips it upside down, and a single piece of old paper floats onto his lap.

"Look. It looks like some sort of journal entry," Roman says.

"Read it," I whisper back. I don't know why we're being so quiet, but it seems right—like we shouldn't be shouting Mary and Samuel's secrets to the world.

"*I've been reunited with my love,*" Roman reads. "*She's nothing but a pillar of fog, but I've found a way to give her strength… to return her to some semblance of the woman she once was. The hag's magic has attached itself to the tree. I was sitting at its trunk, flipping a coin of my father's. I dropped it, and it fell into a small divot in the dirt. I sensed his spirit, though I couldn't see it. He seemed tormented—likely from a life lived in sin. Mary appeared to me again, but this time she was icy flesh and bones. I could touch her, hold her, even push the hair from her face.*

I buried more heirlooms from my family and from those in our community. Mary had color in her cheeks and a smile on her face. When the smile faltered, I'd bury another token to return the sunshine to her skin.

The only thing I've noticed that has changed is her demeanor. She is quick to anger, but that's to be expected in someone who has escaped death's clutches.

I must go now; my bride is waiting in the trees."

"So, you'll come back as a ghost until I bury something to make you solid?" I ask after I let the new information sink in.

Roman shrugs. "I guess so."

"Who knows how many tokens are buried around that tree...and how many of them were put there to keep Mary strong," I say. "She must be really tough by now."

Roman nods and lets out a huge yawn. "My head kinda hurts. Can we watch the movie now?"

"Sure," I say. I know I'm not going to concentrate on the movie with this breakthrough, but Roman looks like he definitely needs a nap.

Roman picks *Spider-Man: Far from Home* and collapses back onto the couch. "Can you grab that blanket?"

I spread a fluffy, green quilt over top of him and sit by his feet. Roman's head tips back a few minutes later, and he's softly snoring before the end of the opening credits. I scoot a little closer to him and pull the blanket over my lap. I take the towel off my head and finger comb the tangles out of my hair as Peter Parker slings his way through Europe.

Roman wakes up with a gasp when the first explosion shakes the room. Jake had insisted on installing special surround sound speakers when their parents redid the rec room. "Why'd you let me sleep?" He grumbles and wipes his eyes. "I missed one of my favorite parts."

"You're supposed to rest," I say. "How else are you going to kick this disease's butt?"

Roman chews on the inside of his lip. "I don't think I'm

going to get better, Els."

My skin crawls so hard my scalp tingles. "But you're getting your stem cell transplant next week. As soon as you kick this disease, you're going to be as good as new."

"I don't know if I'll make it until then." Roman sits up but looks down at the green blanket. "I'm tired, Els. I feel like my body is giving up on me."

The room spins. Everything is going too fast. I squeeze my eyes. This is all just a bad dream. "What can I do to make you feel better?"

Roman nods toward the book. "The only thing you need to do is try to make the Bone Tree work."

"I know," I say.

"But do you promise?" Roman asks.

I nod.

His eyes narrow in an intense way I've never seen before. "Say it."

"If you die—"

Roman shakes his head. "Say *when*, Els."

"When you die—even if it's like fifty years from now, and I need a walker—I'll still hobble back to the Bone Tree to bring you back," I say solemnly.

Roman lets out a long, relieved sigh. "Thanks. Can we nap now?"

"Yeah," I say. "We can sleep now." But I don't nap. I stare at Peter Parker and Mary Jane and wish that life could be like the movies.

—

That night, I dream of the Woman in White. She's hovering above my bed, breathing into my face. It smells like rotten eggs and ashes.

"Why did you take a soul from me?" Her teeth are broken and rotten. Her skin is the color of maggots, and it squirms and twitches like them too.

I thrash and roll, but she's always in front of my face. No matter where I turn, she's always in my face—screaming at me to return the pearl earrings.

Chapter 9

I WON'T FORGET MY PROMISE

NO ONE EVER CALLS AFTER MIDNIGHT WITH GOOD NEWS.
So when the phone rings at 2:57 a.m. three nights after
we watched *Spider-Man*, I know Roman is dead. I wait for
Mom or Dad to come into my room, but they don't. I sit
up and wait for ten whole minutes before I get out of bed. I
can hear them whispering in the kitchen. I tiptoe down the
stairs, somehow knowing that each step I take is one step
closer to no longer having my best friend.

Mom and Dad are huddled in the kitchen. Mom's forehead is resting on Dad's chest. His arms are around her.
They're both crying. I step on the loose kitchen floorboard
on purpose.

My heart feels like it's about to explode. "Is he…?" The
rest of the words won't come out.

"Yes." Mom holds her arms open for me.

"Okay." I don't run into her arms and cry. Tears don't even come. I turn around and walk back up the stairs. I crawl back into my bed and bury my dry face in my pillow.

I don't sleep at all.

—

I didn't cry when I found out Roman died, which is weird considering I've turned into a huge crybaby this past month. But now, five minutes before the funeral starts, I can't stop. I'm in the private viewing room all alone. Roman's wearing the suit his parents bought him for special occasions like Christmas Eve mass and weddings. His hair is what's making me so upset. It's smooth and parted to the side—Roman hates it like that. I want to reach into the polished wooden casket and mess it up a bit, but I'm afraid of what he will feel like.

"Come on," I yell at myself. I wipe a soggy tissue under my eyes and hold by breath to stop the sobs. I reach down, but instead of fixing his hair, I touch Roman's chest. It feels all wrong. He's stiff and still. This cold, hard body can't be my best friend. My knees start to buckle, but before I can fall, someone hauls me back onto my feet.

"The funeral is about to start," Dad says in a low, soft tone. He sounds like he's talking to a freaked-out bird more than his daughter.

I shake my head. "I can't go in there. I can't do this."

"Honey, don't you want to say goodbye?" Mom takes my hand and pulls gently. She looks pretty in her black dress and high heels. I've never willingly worn a dress in my life, so I didn't start today. I'm wearing my black Chuck Taylors, a black jean skirt and a black sweater. Roman wouldn't have cared if I wore a pink tutu, though he might've come back to life just to laugh at me.

"Please don't make me." I wrap my arms around myself and suck back another burst of tears. "It hurts too much."

The tiny side door of the viewing room cracks open and sunshine spills into the room. Jake sticks his head inside. "She can hang out with me if you guys wanna go."

"Son," Dad says. "Don't you think you should be with your family?"

Jake looks at the coffin. "I am."

Mom and Dad leave without another word.

I sit down on the small floral couch reserved for fainting women. Since I can't be trusted to speak without bawling, I don't say anything to Jake. He doesn't say anything to me either. All he does is pace in front of the casket, but he never reaches in.

"Jake?" An older woman pokes her head in. "They're ready for him. I'm going to send in the rest of the boys now."

The rest of the boys?

I force myself to look Jake in the eyes.

He just shrugs. "I wanted to be alone with Roman for a bit."

"I'm sorr—" I start to say, but Jake cuts me off with a stare.

"Don't be sorry. It's easier when you're here." Jake tears his gaze away from me just as a stream of cousins pour through the door. They, along with the funeral home guy, delicately carry away Roman toward the church for the funeral service.

Jake leaves with them, but he's only gone for a few minutes. When he comes back, we go into the parking lot together, and Jake tosses rock after rock at the side of the church. He doesn't go in. I don't go in either. Jake looks older than fourteen right now, especially in his suit. We don't talk at all. We sit on the bumper of a fancy SUV until people spill out of the church doors. I spot Claire Mitchell sandwiched between her parents. Her eyes are red and puffy. She waves at me, but thankfully, she doesn't try to come over. I can't handle any soggy hugs at the moment.

"Don't go anywhere...please. I'll be right back." Jake flicks another rock and goes through the small door into the church. He comes back outside a few minutes later with his cousins and helps load the coffin into the back of a black hearse.

A shiny, black stretch limo is waiting behind the hearse for him and his parents. They climb into it, moving slow and shaky as if they've aged fifty years overnight. Mrs. Pierce is pale and blotchy, wearing a simple black dress. Mr. Pierce is wearing a suit, but it's wrinkled, and his shirt is untucked. This is the picture they should put on those PSAs for not smoking or vaping. This is what happens after you die of cancer—your family crumbles. This is way scarier than messed up lungs.

Jake follows them into the limo and rolls down the window. "Hey Elsie, wanna come with us?"

Mom appears at my side. "Go on. We'll meet you right here when you come back."

I fall into the limo and sit next to Jake. Mrs. Pierce pats my cheek, but she doesn't say anything. Mr. Pierce doesn't even look at me.

We are the only ones to go to the graveyard, aside from the priest. When my grams died the entire family went to the graveyard. The Pierce's didn't want that—they want to say goodbye alone.

Cold wind whips around us, carrying muttered prayers as a machine-operated pulley lowers Roman into the ground. We each get a long-stemmed white rose to toss into the hole.

"I won't forget my promise," I whisper as I let go of the flower.

Cold wind howls in my ear, as though Mary and the Bone Tree are screaming, *"We see you."*

—

Mom lets me stay home from school the next week. Even though I don't have to wake up early, I go to bed the same time every night, and each night I wake up at eleven on the dot. I stand up—still dressed in my clothes from the day—and sneak onto the roof. Sometimes I sit on the roof for an hour, imaging the exact route to the Bone Tree before I go back inside. Other times I jump off and make it into the backyard before I scale the tree and climb back inside through my window. No matter how many times I try, I can't make myself walk out of my back gate.

—

When I do go back to school, I'm ambushed by crowds of *I'm sorry*, and *You can talk to me*. No matter where I go, around every corner waits a concerned teacher or a tear-stained friend. I try to ignore everyone, but it feels like they can't stop being sad until they tell me how sad they are. So I let them hug me and cry. I take their inspirational Hallmark cards and eat the treats their moms send for me. I do all of this for Roman, even though I hate every second of it.

I'm not a loser. I have friends besides Roman. I mean, we had friends other than each other. Sometimes we went to movie night at Ashleigh Hackett's house. Other nights we went to the twins', Carlee and Levi Mercer, to hang out in their huge game room. But we, Roman and I, were never really *I's*. Roman never went to Ashleigh's without me, and I haven't been to a game night since Roman got sick.

Now I'm the only half of the *we* left.

Now I'm just an *I*.

When Ashleigh invites me over to watch the newest scary movie on the latest streaming service, my parents think I should go.

I tell Ashleigh I'm not allowed.

When Levi sticks a note in my locker, filling me in on the ping pong tournament going down in their game room, I pretend I didn't see it.

Being an *I* is too hard. I'd really rather be nothing at all.

The day our math teacher accidentally calls out Roman's name during attendance, I lose it. I leave my books and run out of the classroom. I can't breathe. I run in aimless loops through hallways until a figure steps through the open library door. It's Ms. Young.

"Come in." Her voice is calm and steady—none of the wavery bits of everyone else trying not to cry.

I run into the library and stop at the tiny cubicle closest to Ms. Young's giant desk. I suck in breath after breath of musty air until my heart slows down, and I feel human again.

"I'm sorry," I say, even though I don't have any reason to apologize.

Ms. Young opens a thermos and pours steaming liquid into the lid. She sets it on the little desk in the cubicle. It smells like peppermint.

"Someone told me this a long, long time ago, so it may not apply to your situation, but it's best received with a cup of tea." Ms. Young nods at the tiny cup in front of me. "Losing someone feels like the worst possible storm—at first it's a tornado. It tears up your entire life and sucks the air from your lungs. It consumes you. It is impossible to ignore. Then one day, without you realizing it, it's the most vicious thunderstorm, only the thunder strikes a little less often. The wind is a touch more tolerable. It's scary and it breaks things, but we recover faster. Next time, you see the dark clouds coming. You have time to prepare. You close the windows and put your bike in the shed…you know what the storm is going to bring. It still hurts—it will always hurt—but you know what you need to do to survive. Eventually you look forward to the fall thunderstorms…you smile when the thunder booms because it reminds you of their smile and the way they smell and their favorite movie. Yes, there is a part of your heart that still aches when the rain comes, but it gets easier. It feels impossible now, Elsie, but I promise, you can weather this storm."

I sip the tea as tears just as warm pour down my face. This doesn't feel like something I can handle, but maybe one day it will. I finish my tea and wipe my face. Ms. Young doesn't say anything. She takes her empty cup back and smiles a little as I walk out of the library, my face dry.

—

For the first few weeks, Mom and Dad were really patient. They didn't get mad when I went straight to bed after school. They even let me eat supper in my room.

Now, not so much. Tonight, Mom lets out a sigh when I sit at the table in my fleece cow jammies.

"I'm glad you fixed up for us," she says as she sets a roasted chicken in the middle of the table.

"Carla, don't start this," Dad says. "She's trying."

Mom rubs her eyes. "I'm sorry, honey. Just eat your dinner and go back to bed."

I eat, but I don't go to bed. I get dressed, and I sit on the roof with a flashlight in one hand and the baggie of Roman in the other.

—

When I come home from school the next day, Mom is waiting for me in my room.

"Hey," I say. "Whatcha doing in here?"

Mom spreads the lumps out of my comforter. "I was waiting for you. Ashleigh's mom called. They're going to the amusement park tomorrow, and she was wondering if you wanted to—"

"No, that's okay," I say before Mom can finish.

"Honey, it might be nice for you to spend some time with your friends." Mom smiles–it's the same sad smile I get from everyone else, only this one is mixed with a little something else. Fear, I think. She looks at me like she's afraid that I'm going to leave the house, but she's also scared that I won't. I wish I could tell her that I'm going to be okay, but I'm not sure I ever will be okay again.

"I said I don't want to go." I grab my pajamas from my drawer. "Can you get out? I need to change."

"Elsie," Mom snaps. "I know you miss Roman. We all do, but it's been three weeks since you've done anything. I'm getting worried."

"I'm fine, Mom," I say. "I just don't want to go to a dumb kiddie place, that's all."

"You need to see your other friends—"

A tidal wave of anger splashes over me. "I don't want my other friends!" I scream. "I want Roman!"

I grab my hoodie with the baggie in it and run down the hallway. Mom shouts after me, but I ignore her.

I take my bike I never used, since Roman had the pegs on his, and pedal away as fast as I can. I make it to the cemetery in record time. Before I can change my mind, I sprint down the twisty path until I come to the Bone Tree.

Even with the sun shining on it, the tree is still creepy. Maybe it's because I know there's bits and pieces of a dead body buried deep below. I get on my knees and dig with my bare hands. The dirt is damp from this morning's frost and cold chunks of it creep under my fingernails, but I keep digging until I have a skinny, deep hole. I grab the baggie with Roman's blood and hair in it and toss it into the ground, cover the hole and wait. Nothing happens. There's no icy breeze, no howling, no Roman, no nothing.

It's just me, the abandoned *I*, and the Bone Tree.

Chapter 10
ROMAN

I FALL ASLEEP EARLY AND DREAM OF ROMAN JUST LIKE I have the last twenty-two nights. Usually, in my dream, we're at school or his house, stretched out on the couch watching movies in the rec room. Tonight, we're in the graveyard. Well, I'm there, Roman is somewhere in the trees. He waves to me through the branches, his pale arms blending in with the birch tree limbs. Each time I catch up to him, he disappears. I chase him to the Bone Tree and find him hanging upside down on one of the branches.

"Hey," I say, even though Roman never talks back in my dream.

Roman flashes me a goofy grin. His mouth forms the words, "Hey, yourself."

I kick a rock and it bounces into the empty hole we dug

the pearl earrings up from. I sit down on the dirt and stare up at Roman. "I miss you."

He swings down and sits next to me. He drags his fingers in the dirt, turning lines into letters.

I read them out loud. "I'm back…"

Roman nods so fast his features blur together. His mouth becomes a black, gaping hole. He looks like he's living in the space between camera flashes—all glitches and snaps of color. It sends shivers down my spine, but I make myself ignore the fear—this is Roman. He stops nodding and opens his mouth, silently shouting—only it's not so silent anymore. "Echoooooooooooo."

I wake up, panting as if it's track and field day all over again. My room is so quiet that it plugs my ears, and all I can hear is the rabbit stuck inside my chest. The broken streetlight is still broken, so it's pitch black in my room. That is until my walkie wakes up from its twenty-two night nap and static takes over.

"Echooooooooo." The words fill the air like a long, sleepy sigh.

I grab the walkie and press it against my ear. A chill swirls around me, but it isn't icy or scary. It feels like a blast of air conditioning on a sticky summer day.

"Liiimma," the walkie yawns.

The voice is so familiar it hurts. I hold my breath and wait for it to continue.

"Echooo." Static crackles and fizzes. "Liimma."

The side button is warm under my fingers as if someone had just been pressing it. "Romeo Oxford, come in."

Silence.

"Roman?" I squeeze my eyes shut and wait for him to say something, anything, to let me know he's here.

The walkie crackles a few more times, but no one answers. I look out the window into the backyard, but no one is there. My heart drops, and a wave of sadness wells up in my chest and threatens to pour out of my eyes. I flop onto my side and wedge the walkie between my pillow and my ear— just in case.

I stare into the darkness and think about Roman, as usual. In my dreams, he looks like normal Roman, but in the ground, buried under the dirt, I know he looks like something much, much worse. I made the mistake of googling what a body would look like after three weeks underground.

By now, his internal organs have started to rot. His body has already bloated, pushing bloody foam out of his nose and mouth. His decomposing organs have caused giant amounts of gas to fill his body—his skin turning from green to red.

I shudder when I think about Roman's skin turning colors. If I waited another month, his teeth and fingernails will fall out.

What will I do if Roman looks like a zombie rather than my friend? My teeth chatter so hard my head aches. I squeeze my eyes shut and focus on the white noise pouring out of the walkie-talkie, desperate for a sign that Roman is still Roman.

I wake up early for a Saturday, and my heart hurts all over again as if someone picked the Roman-sized scab that was just starting to heal.

Mom knocks on the door and waltzes in.

"Mom," I groan. "What if I was naked?"

Mom rests an empty laundry basket on her hip and starts tossing clothes into it. "It's nothing I haven't seen before."

I sit up enough to grab my pillow out from underneath my head. Before I can smother myself, my head meets something hard and plastic. I yelp and grab the back of my head with one hand and the plastic weapon with the other. "Son of a—"

"Watch it," Mom says as her eyes narrow into Iron Man slits.

"I was gonna say *bee sting*." I look down at the walkie—now on the ground—just as it crackles again. I yelp. In my hand is an unpackaged limited-edition Venom action figure—the same one that used to sit on Roman's cluttered shelf.

I pull on jeans, skip the bathroom and run out the door before Mom has time to blink. I hop on my bike and, for the first time in twenty-three days, I smile. I smile so big my cheeks ache, and I get a gnat in my teeth as my bike and I soar toward the cemetery. I toss my bike onto the grass and clear the iron fence in one huge jump. I run down the now-worn path to the Bone Tree.

"Roman!" I rub my sore cheeks and search for my friend. "Where are you?"

The only answer I get is from a ticked off squirrel chattering at me from a nearby branch. I wander through the trees, careful not to walk too close to the crumbling headstones, and search for Roman.

"Please be here." I shuffle through piles of crunchy leaves and scratchy sticks, but I can't find him anywhere. I should've known it wouldn't have been that easy. Maybe I made the whole thing up in my head. Roman's parents gave me a box of his stuff, and the action figure could've been in there. Maybe I was sleepwalking last night and grabbed it. Maybe Roman's not back after all.

Suddenly the skin on the back of my neck prickles like someone is watching me. I whirl around and shout, "Roman?"

There's no one here, but the feeling won't go away. I take a few steps backward until I step into a patch of air so cold my entire body gets goose bumps. Then my stomach starts to hurt. It hurts as if I ate a week's worth of gas station sushi all at once. The pain swirls in my belly, up my throat and into my brain. I grab the sides of my head as it begins to pound. Even though the cemetery is silent, it sounds like someone is screaming at the top of their lungs, right into my ear.

Leave. Leave. Leave.

I scramble back down the path, tripping over roots and old gravestones until I'm back at my bike. The farther I get away from the Bone Tree, the less everything hurts. By the time I start to pedal, all the pain is gone.

What the heck?

I've seen enough episodes of *Supernatural* to know that spirits have ways of communicating with people, even if they don't make a peep. If they think a little chilly air and a headache is going to keep me away from my best friend, they have another thing coming.

I take a shortcut through the park near my house even though bikes aren't allowed on the walking paths. A group of high school kids are sprawled out on the benches lining the path. I wish for the millionth time that Roman was with me; he would take us down another path without seeming like a chicken. But Roman isn't here, and I'm not going to let the older kids think I'm afraid of them, even though I am. I suck in a chilly breath of air and pedal into the sea of skinny jeans and knit hats.

"Out for a bike ride before your mommy drops you off at daycare?" a girl who looks at least sixteen sneers.

"Shut up," I mutter. I stand up on the pedals and shove all my weight down. I get one good burst of speed before my chain falls off. I steer into the grass and push my bike over to a little cluster of trees, ignoring the chipmunk sounding laughter. I lean my bike against the widest trunk and crouch down.

"Did you forget your training wheels?" another kid shouts.

"Shut up, shut up, shut up," I say to the greasy chain. I slip it back over the gears and wipe my fingers on the grass.

"Need some help?" someone asks from behind me.

I stand up and come face to chest with a tall, lanky boy. I look up and see a black hood circling a familiar face. "It's you!"

But it's not.

Jake pushes back his black hoodie and shakes out his straw-colored hair. "Yeah, it's me."

My heart falls to my feet. "I thought you were someone else."

"Sorry I'm such a disappointment." Jake walks back to the path with me. "I haven't seen you in a while."

"There's not really a point in coming over anymore," I say as I climb onto my bike.

Jake grabs my arm and tugs me a little closer. He smells like the fruity cigarettes the high school kids' smoke. "Mom and Dad would like it. They miss you. You're kinda like a little sister."

"They don't miss me, they miss Roman." I stare up at Jake and try to swallow around the baseball-sized lump in my throat. His eyes are full of red spider webs. "Are you okay? You look a little…weird."

Jake sways and lets go of my arm. "Don't worry about it. I forget sometimes that you're just a kid."

This hurts more than the training wheels comment. "Yeah, well you're just a jerk."

I shove off the pavement, and this time my bike agrees with me. I speed all the way home and kick the back door open. I shove my shoes off my feet and stomp upstairs.

"Elsie Edwards, where have you been?" Mom stands in the middle of the living room with her cell phone in one hand and her hip in the other.

"I forgot I had to go pick up something at Ashleigh's." I duck so she can't see the lie on my face.

"I was going to call there next." Mom sighs. "You can't go running off like that without telling me where you're going. I know Fredric Falls is a small town, but we did have that one murder six years ago."

"That was actually ten years ago, and it wasn't even in town." I sit down at the dinner table. "But I'm sorry. I should have checked in."

"We need to put that tracking app on your phone." Mom sets an egg sandwich down in front of me.

"Whatever." I'm definitely not in the mood for this talk again. I take a huge bite of my breakfast.

Mom shakes her head. "Dad and I are going out for dinner tonight, will you be okay alone? I can ask someone to pop in if you want?"

"I don't need a babysitter," I say around a mouthful of gooey cheese.

"Can you behave on your own for that long?" Mom arches an eyebrow at me.

"I forgot I have homework, so I'll be doing that all night anyway."

I don't tell Mom that my homework is code for best-friend-ghost-hunting.

—

As soon as Mom and Dad leave, I get dressed for the cold and turn on my walkie. I sit on the floor next to my shoe rack and wait for Roman to talk to me. This time I'm not giving him enough time to disappear on me. Five minutes after the sun sets, and the streetlamps flicker on, a bubble of static comes out of the small speaker. "Echooo" is all I hear before I drop the walkie, burst out through the front door, get on my bike and fly.

I speed over speed bumps and swerve around potholes. I count to one hundred and try to slow my heart down. My mouth won't top switching between a smile and a frown. I want to laugh and cry at the same time.

What will I do if Roman isn't there at all?

I shake the thought from my head. Roman will be there. He has to be. I pedal faster, leaves kicking up around my tires like tiny tornados. I didn't believe Roman when he first told me about the Bone Tree. Now the legend is the only thing that makes me want to get out of bed. When I reach the familiar iron fence that borders the cemetery, I practically leap off my bike and hurdle over the fence as fast as I can.

The graveyard is empty, but I know something is there. This time, it's a good something. The air smells like fresh laundry, and my heart doesn't feel like someone is using it as a punching bag.

"I know you're here, Roman." I thump my chest with my fist. It's gone from racing fast to super slow. "I can feel you."

A familiar chuckle drifts over the tombstones and curls around the Bone Tree.

"Where are you?" I run around the white, smooth tree trunk, but I can't see him. A breeze lifts my hair off my neck.

"Hey, Els," Roman whispers.

"Roman!" I whirl around, hoping he's real.

He stands behind me, pale as a cloud, but here. I launch myself at him, but I fall right through him and land on the ground. "You're here."

"Sure am." Roman looks down at me. Our faces are only inches apart. He looks so real I can hardly believe it.

I scramble up from the ground, but I keep staring. Messy black hair, bright blue eyes, faded Superman T-shirt underneath a red zip-up hoodie. He looks normal, just a little hazy as if I'm staring at him through Saran wrap. Big, fat, happy tears roll down my cheeks. "It's really you."

Roman grins. "It's really me. Can you believe the Bone Tree really worked?"

I smile and then smack my forehead. "I totally forgot to bring something to bury for your energy. I'm sorry…you're going to be all misty and stuff for a while longer."

"It's okay. You can bring it next time." Roman ducks his head and stares into my eyes. "If you want too, I mean. You don't have to come back. I know this place freaks you out."

"This could be the scariest place in the whole world, and I'd still come back." Usually I'd punch him in the shoulder after saying something this mushy, but it wouldn't work even if I tried. "What was it like on the uh, other side?"

Roman opens his mouth, but no words come out. He tries again, his mouth twisting into funny faces. His face shakes a little as he tries to speak. "Weird, I want to tell you, but I can't."

"I won't tell anyone," I say. "Promise."

"No, like I physically can't." Roman traces odd shapes in the dirt. They start off looking like letters, but they morph into weird, squiggly shapes halfway through. "I can't spell it out either."

"Seriously?" I look at the funny shapes again.

"Yeah, it must be some afterlife gag order." Roman shrugs.

"Who knew security was so tight up there." My cell buzzes, letting me know its ten o'clock already.

"Do you need to go?" Roman asks.

"Yeah, my parents will be home soon." I stand up and stretch. "Can you come with me?"

Roman flashes me a sideways smile. "I can try."

We make it to the fence. Roman starts to flicker out.

"I think this is as far as I can go without a token," Roman says. "I'll see you tomorrow?"

"I'll be here as soon as the sun goes down," I reply as I grab my bike and hop on. "As long as my parents don't bust me, that is."

"Hey, Els," Roman says.

I turn around and look at him. I still can't believe he's here. "Yeah?"

"Thanks for bringing me back."

I give him my biggest smile. "Anytime."

Chapter 11

GRANDMA'S JEWELRY

"ELSIE, SUPPER'S READY!" MOM CALLS FROM DOWNSTAIRS.

"I'm coming!" I yell back. I'm in Mom's bedroom, digging around in my Grams's jewelry for something to bring to Roman. My Grams died, and my mom uses her jewelry for special occasions.

"I'm sorry to do this, Mom, but it's for a good cause." I take the plainest, smallest piece I can find; a set of tiny, black dangling earrings with heads carved out of white rock. She'll never notice they're gone. I carefully rearrange the jewelry to hide the newly formed gap and rush downstairs to the kitchen before Mom yells at me again.

"How was school today?" Dad asks when I sit down at the table.

"It was good," I say, even though I hardly remember going

to any of my classes, let alone if they were good or not. I've spent the whole day wishing the sun would go down already.

Mom sets down a bubbling hot lasagna and sits next to me. "I ran into Mrs. Pierce at the grocery store this morning. She wants you to come for a visit."

"Maybe I'll go after school one day," I say. "Do you think it'll be weird?"

Mom shakes her head. "If something ever happened to you, I'd want to be around anything and anyone that reminded me of you. Not that anything is going to happen to you, of course."

"Hey, premature death and pasta don't go together," Dad says. He hates talking about sad stuff, especially sad stuff involving Roman. Sometimes I think Dad misses Roman just as much as I do. "Now how about that girl band scandal, or whatever."

Mom and Dad take turns showing how little they know about any cool famous people while we eat. Once we're done with dinner, I watch TV with them for an hour or so before faking a yawn.

"Ugh, I'm so tired lately." I stretch out on the couch and rub my eyes.

"It's because it's getting so dark so early," Mom says. "You'll perk up in no time."

"I hope so." I stand up and yawn again. "I'm going to bed. Night."

"Night," Mom and Dad say in unison.

I have a feeling that Dad's going to check on me tonight. So instead of jetting out at nine, like I really want to, I go to my bedroom and stay there. At ten, just after his favorite show ends, he pokes his head into my room. I stay as still as a board with my eyes glued shut. My door shuts a few seconds later, and Dad slips down the hallway. I give him and Mom a few minutes to settle in, and then I'm gone.

—

When I get to the Bone Tree, Roman is legit hovering in front of it.

"Elsie!" Roman zooms up to his feet.

"Neat trick," I say. "I thought I'd dreamt it the whole night."

"Me too," Roman says. "Except I don't sleep."

I sit down on a stump and look around the woods. "What do you do all day?"

Roman sprawls out next to my feet and props his head up with his hand. "Climbed a few trees and explored a little. The day went by so fast."

"I wish my day passed like that," I say. "I was stuck in school all day. I wish you could come."

"Can I ask you a weird question?" Roman effortlessly pulls himself onto a low-hanging branch.

"Depends," I say. "Was that it?"

"Ha, ha." Roman rolls his eyes. "What was my funeral like?"

"Uh, it was nice." I grab my braid and wrap it around my finger. "Really nice."

Roman flings himself off the branch and hovers an inch away from my face. "Elsie Edwards, you little liar. You skipped my funeral, didn't you?"

I look down and dig my toe into the ground. "I tried going, honestly I did, but it was too hard. We went to the wake, but we skipped the church."

Roman blinks. "We? My brother skipped it too?"

"I'm sorry," I whisper.

"I'm not mad at you, dummy," he says. "I'm happy you stayed with Jake. How's he doing?"

I think about telling him the truth—that Jake doesn't seem good at all—but I change my mind at the last minute and lie. I'll give Jake another chance to act like a normal human before I worry Roman. "He's sad, but he seems to be doing good. He's not getting into fist fights or getting expelled or anything."

At least I hope not.

"That's good," he says. "What about my parents?"

I shrug guiltily. "I haven't seen them since your funeral. Your mom invited me over, so I'll go real soon. I promise."

"Tell them I say hi." Roman lets out a sad little laugh. "So, did you bring me something?"

"I sure did." I kneel down and dig a few inches down in the dirt. I reach into my pocket, careful of the pokey backs, and pull out the earrings. "Do you think I need to tell the tree that I'm burying these for your strength, not Mary's?"

Roman shrugs. "Maybe say that the earrings are for my energy, not Mary Simon's."

I hold the earrings up to my mouth. "These are to give Roman strength and keep him here with me." I drop the earrings and cover them with dirt and leaves.

Please let this work.

"Now what?" Roman floats around the tree.

"I dunno. Do you feel different?"

"Not really." And then he disappears.

My heart plummets to my feet. "Roman!" My voice cracks. He can't be gone. I just got him back. I gulp in as much air as I can, squeeze my eyes shut and scream. "Roman!"

"Hey!" Roman appears from behind the Bone Tree.

"You scared me, you jerk." I pull my elbow back and drive my fist into his arm as hard as I can. He's solid—so solid that it feels like I'm punching a block of ice. "Owww!"

I sandwich my hand between my knees and blink back fire-hot tears. I knew he'd be more solid, but I didn't think he'd be as hard as a rock.

"Are you okay?" Roman pulls my hand free and holds it up to his face. "Why'd you hit me so hard? You could have broken something…of yours, not mine."

"Because you deserved it," I growl. "Don't scare me like that ever again."

"I won't." Roman pats my hand. "I promise."

A terrible cry fills the air. I grab Roman's sleeve. "Do you think Mary is coming?"

"I don't know, Els, but get ready to run." Roman squints down the path. "I think it's a ghost. You should get out of here. She could be dangerous."

"I'm not leaving without you." I grab his other sleeve. I clench my jaw and turn toward the sound. If Mary is coming, I'm not going to run. I'm going to stay and fight for Roman. A pillar of fog materializes between the trees in front of us. I take in a deep breath and dig my feet into the dirt.

Give it your best shot, Mary.

A woman steps—more like staggers—out of the fog. She's all wispy and blurry, but it's definitely a woman. She falls against a tree first and then to her knees. She clutches her chest and then falls sideways. Her feet twitch and then all her breath rushes out in a cloud.

"Did she just fall asleep?" I ask.

Roman takes a step closer. "I think she just died."

"Oh." The fear in my stomach turns to sadness.

Roman leans a little closer to the extra-dead ghost. "How did your Grams die?"

"She had a heart attack," I say. "Why?"

The ghost stirs and sits up slowly as though she's just waking up.

"Don't look." Roman spins around and covers my eyes. "I'm so sorry, Elsie."

I grab his wrist and pull his hand down. "What are you talking about?"

The ghost falls again. She's closer now, close enough that I can see her face. I can see red seeping from her mouth as her teeth clamp down on her lip. I watch her skin break as her nails dig into her chest. She groans and falls to her knees—I fall too.

"Grams?" I whisper. I reach for her, but my hand passes right through her. She bucks against the unmoving leaves. "Roman, help!" I cry.

Roman sits next to me. "I can't do anything, I'm sorry, Elsie. I'm so sorry."

"Tell me what to do, Grams." I suck back the sob waiting to escape. "How do I make it stop?"

"Dig the earrings up," Grams gasps. "It hurts so much. Please, dig up the token."

Grams gnarled hand slides against the ground in the direction of the Bone Tree.

"The earrings!" I scramble to the tree and dig up the fresh hole. I stop before I grab the earrings. "What will this do to you, Roman?"

Roman shakes his head. "I don't know, but it doesn't matter. Grab the earrings, Els."

Grams shudders and dies again. I choke on a sob as a part of me dies too. I can't believe this is what happens to the token's owners. I feel so terrible, my stomach aches. I grab the earrings and jam them into my pocket. The pointed end digs into my middle finger, but I don't care. I crawl back toward Grams, leaving a miniature trail of blood behind me. She stands to her feet, but this time she doesn't fall.

"I'm so sorry, Grams," I say, not bothering to swipe at my falling tears. "I never would've buried your earrings if I knew this would happen."

"It's all right, child." Gram's faint British accent soothes my racing heart. "The pain is gone."

"Are more ghosts like you suffering?" I ask, scanning the woods around us.

Grams closes her eyes and nods. "When a token is buried, a spirit is forced to relive their death—the energy of their agony feeds the one bound to the Bone Tree…Mary, or as she's known as…the Woman in White."

A thick fog rolls toward us, more and more bodies form the closer it gets. They tumble and fall onto the ground, their mouths gaping open. And then the screaming begins.

It starts off with a single high-pitched wail. A female ghost slips, her arms wind-milling like she's falling, and then the scream stops as her entire body jerks like she just hit the ground—but she doesn't because she's floating. She is still for a moment before she starts to cry out again, arms waving, and then nothing.

The man next to her coughs, clutching at his throat, and then gurgles until his pale, ghostly face turns blue. He falls forward, but his heavy body leaves the dried leaves underneath him silent.

All around me, ghosts moan and shout as they die over and over again. I want to cover my ears and run away, but I can't leave Grams and Roman. This is worse than any scary movie I've ever seen. This is real.

"What can I do?" I whisper, tears stabbing my eyes from both fear and sadness. I reach for Grams, but before I can touch her, she disappears in a shock of bright light. The ghosts vanish, and then I'm all alone. I spin around and search for Roman.

"Roman?" I call out. He isn't behind me. "Roman! You promised you wouldn't hide from me, remember?"

Silence.

I run around the Bone Tree, but I can't find him. I collapse into the leaves and twigs and unleash a tidal wave of tears. I faintly notice the trail of blood I left, now disappearing into the ground.

Chapter 12

HALF A HEART

I TRY TO LEAVE THE CEMETERY—ALL I WANT TO DO IS hide under my covers for the rest of my life—but I can't leave Roman. Instead of leaving, I walk along the outside of the graveyard until I wind up on a cement path. I could go the rest of the way with my eyes closed, but I don't.

I head for Roman's grave and stifle a yelp when I see someone is already there. Jake is sitting on the ground with his back against the tall, marble headstone—since I'm standing in the shadows, he can't see me. He tosses a hacky sack in the air over and over again. He doesn't catch it and instead lets the worn, woolen bag of rice hit the brown grass and picks it up again.

"Mom and Dad miss you. They've stopped crying every day, at least in front of me, but I know they're still wrecked. We all are. Elsie is having a hard time...she acts like you might come back one day. You should still be here." Jake tosses the hacky sack in the air once more before he buries his face in his arms.

I can't leave him alone to cry, so I walk until I'm at Roman's grave. I sit down on the other side and rest the back of my head on the cool stone. I run my hands over the dried bunch of flowers and pluck away the petals.

I want to tell Jake that he doesn't need to cry. That Roman was sort of alive, and up until a half an hour ago, Jake could've seen him for himself. But I can't tell him any of that, not anymore. I look up at the gigantic moon and make all my birthday wishes in a row. I wish Roman would show up right now and fix our broken hearts. I wish Jake's parents could have seen that Roman is back, even if it were just for a little while. Most of all, I wish Roman didn't die in the first place.

A thousand tears later, Jake takes a deep breath and climbs to his feet. He comes around to my side of the grave and pulls me up to my feet. Jake doesn't ask why I'm here in the cemetery in the middle of the night. He probably thinks I was here to do the same thing he was. All he does is nudge me with his elbow and says, "Let's go, Elsie."

I follow Jake down the path. "You can call me Els, you know. Everyone else does."

Jake shakes his head. "No, I can't. That's what Roman called you. Every night it was, 'Els and I are going to the movies' or 'Els said the funniest thing in class today.' It's just…too Roman."

I swallow hard. "I get it."

Once we get out of the cemetery, Jake picks up his bike. "Where's your wheels?"

"I left my bike at home. It's too suspicious if my parents get home and notice it's gone," I say.

"I better get you home before you turn into a pumpkin then," Jake says.

"Look who's talking, nine o'clock curfew," I shoot back.

Jake's ears turn just pink enough to make me smile. "Get on already."

"I'm not going to sit on your handlebars like the girls you're always hanging out with," I say.

"You can ride on the back." Jake nods at the purple pegs—the ones Roman put on his bike for me—sticking out of the back tire. "Roman gave these to me before he uh, left."

"Oh…okay." I climb onto the pegs and grab the bar under Jake's seat, careful not to touch any scrap of Jake's jeans. I don't ever want to touch a boy's butt, especially not Jake's. Even if he does smell like peppermint.

"You're going to fall if you hold on like that." Jake reaches back and puts my hand up onto his shoulder.

I hold onto him, but just barely. I do squeeze a little tighter once Jake pushes off the pavement.

Riding with Jake is different than Roman. Roman was all smooth-sailing; he'd gently loop around the potholes and warn me of all the speed bumps. Jake pedals like we're being chased by the cops. He purposely hits the potholes, and my teeth knock together each time.

"Speed bump's coming up," Jake says.

I cling to Jake's shoulders, and for just one second, we're as weightless as Thor soaring up to Asgard.

—

After Jake drops me off and pedals away, I make it back inside my house without waking my parents up. I change into my jammies and wash my face with icy, cold water. My eyes are all puffy from crying. I climb into bed and pull the covers up to my chin. Everything hurts all over again. The floorboards in the hallway squeak. I close my eyes just as Mom cracks the door open.

Her breath catches in her throat. "Oh, Elsie."

Soft footsteps cross the floor, and my mattress tilts under her weight. Cool fingers brush my forehead.

"I thought she was getting better," Mom whispers.

"She is," Dad says. I didn't even hear him walk in.

"No." Mom sighs and traces my eyes with the tip of her fingers. "Her eyes are swollen. She's been crying, babe, and not just a little bit. These are up-all-night eyes."

"Maybe we need to bring her to a therapist?" Dad's voice is thick. "Maybe it'd be good for us all to go as a family."

"Maybe." Mom sighs again. "I hope she pulls through this...I hope we all do."

I can practically hear her tears falling. I should wake up and lie to her face. I should tell her that I'm okay, but

I'm not. Nothing is okay anymore. Maybe I'll never be okay again.

"Let's go to bed before we wake her," Dad says.

Mom brushes a kiss along my cheek. "We'll get through this, baby girl. I promise."

I wait until Mom and Dad are gone before I roll onto my side and bury my face in my pillow. I think about Grams and the pain she was in all because of me. I think about Roman disappearing again. If he truly is gone, I don't see how anything Mom says could possibly be true.

Chapter 13
THE DEAD'S ENERGY

I DREAM ABOUT THE BONE TREE THAT SAME NIGHT, BUT this time Roman's not here. I race up and down the trails and around the Bone Tree, but he never shows up. I step into a puddle and can actually feel the icy water circling my ankles. Suddenly, I'm wide awake and landing on the floor—butt first. Moonlight trickles in from my bedroom window, bathing my fuzzy carpet in cool, white light.

"Whoops, sorry, Els." Roman kneels in front of me. "Are you okay?"

"Roman?" I throw myself into his arms. "How are you here right now?"

"Am I still dreaming?"

Roman grins and stands up with me still in his arms. "You're not dreaming, Els. I'm here. I don't really understand how. When I disappeared, everything was extremely bright. Like the sun bright, but times a thousand. I thought for a second that I was crossing over, or whatever, but nothing happened. I just stayed in this mega ball of light until every inch of me was glowing. Then I panicked because I thought I was going to explode."

"Did you?" He seems like he's in one piece, but you can't be too sure with ghost friends. I flick on my lamp and stare at him; he looks normal, still-dead-but-not-really kind of normal. I've never been so happy to see anyone in my entire life.

"Nope." Roman sits next to me on the bed. The mattress squeaks under his solid but ghostly weight.

Strange.

"Right when I couldn't take anymore, I woke up lying next to the Bone Tree. I started to walk, and when I reached the fence line, I just kept walking. I didn't get weak or anything, even though I don't have any tokens buried."

I pinch Roman's arm just to double-check that he's solid.

Roman bats my hand away and rises a few inches off the bed. "Try that now."

I reach up, but my hand passes right through him.

"Cool, hey?" Roman asks. "It must be a ghostly trick of the trade."

A knock comes at my door, and Dad comes in just as Roman floats even higher.

I jump up and hold out my arms to hide Roman, not that my twiggy arms could actually hide anything. I hold my breath and wait for Dad to freak out.

Instead, Dad holds up his hand to block the lamp's light and squints at me. "What are you doing up? It's three in the morning."

I look up at Roman and then back down at Dad again. "Uh, I had a bad dream, that's all."

I give Dad another chance to turn the color of my freshly washed sheets and faint or call for an exorcist, but he doesn't do anything.

"Do you need a glass of water?" Dad asks. "Or some milk?"

"No, I'm okay. I'll just go back to bed." I lie back down and pull the covers back over me.

Dad comes and sits on the edge of the bed, right under Roman's dangling feet. "What were you dreaming about? Roman?"

Oh, great.

"Not this time," I say. "I think I was dreaming about giant bugs chasing me."

Dad takes one look at my anxious face and sighs. "You don't have to lie to me. I miss him too, Elsie."

"I know," I say.

Roman drifts down, so he's hovering right next to Dad. He reaches out to touch him, but I shoot him a look not to.

Dad looks at Roman—well, through Roman—and sighs. "Anyways, you should go back to sleep."

"Night, Dad," I say.

"Night, pumpkin." Dad yawns and shuts the door.

As soon as his footsteps get quieter and quieter, Roman

crashes onto the bed. He solidifies at the last second, and my headboard smacks against the wall.

"I just banged my head!" I shout before punching Roman's shoulder. "You're not air anymore. You need to be careful."

Roman rubs his shoulder even though I'm positive it didn't hurt. "Why can't your Dad see me?"

"I have no idea," I say. I can't make sense of any of it, really.

"Did you go see my parents yet?"

"Uh, not yet. Jake invited me, so I think I'll go someday soon." I pick at the sleeve of my pajama shirt.

"You and Jake are hanging out now?" Roman rubs his nose even though there aren't any glasses on it to push up.

"Not really. I bumped into him right after I snuck out." It's awkward talking to Roman about Jake, and I don't know why. It's like when Mom and Dad both bake cookies and make me choose whose I like best.

"Hmm." Roman makes the same face he used to whenever his mom put kale in his smoothie. "How is he?"

"Sad."

"That's it?" Roman asks.

I shrug. "He's really, really sad." I nibble my nail and hiss when my teeth bite the tiny puncture wound on my finger.

"You okay?" Roman asks.

"Yeah. I accidentally stabbed myself with my Grams's earrings before you disappeared."

Roman taps his finger against his lips. "Did it bleed?"

"A little," I say. "Why?"

Roman hops up and starts to pace. "This all makes sense now."

I chuck a pillow at him. "What are you talking about?"

"When I was in the light, I kept smelling daisies like that body spray you and all the girls in our class wear." Roman stops walking and points at me. "When I woke up, I felt like I needed to get to you right away. I can't explain it—I just needed to be where you were. Maybe your blood acted like a dead person's ring or something? Maybe that's why I don't need any tokens to keep me here!"

"And why I'm the only one that can see you?" I ask. "And if the Bone Tree uses the dead's energy, or something, right? If you were using mine, wouldn't I be able to feel it?"

Roman shrugs and flashes me a gigantic smile. "I guess only time will tell. You should stock up on power bars and vitamins just in case."

"I'll make sure my mom puts that on the grocery list." I look at my old-school alarm clock and hold back a yawn. "Now what?"

"Now you go to sleep, and I'll catch up on *Supernatural*." Roman grabs my laptop and shoves me over. "Night, Els."

"Night, Roman."

I fall asleep after only a few seconds. It feels as though everything is right back to the way it used to be.

Chapter 14

HOW DO YOU KNOW?

I HARDLY SLEEP A WINK, EVEN THOUGH ROMAN IS RIGHT beside me. Each time I doze off, I dream that Roman is gone, and I'm alone again. I wish there were some sort of rulebook or webpage I could research instead of living every second wondering when Roman is going to vanish again.

When I finally fall asleep, I only get a couple hours before Mom is yelling at me to come downstairs and start my day, even though we don't have school today. It's one of those random Monday holidays. Roman decides to go test out his floating abilities so I can get dressed. When I walk into the kitchen, I think I spot him next to the fridge. Only it isn't him—it's another ghost.

Dread fills my stomach. What the heck is it doing here?

A tall, dark man is looming over my mother. He isn't touching her, but he's close. *Too close.*

"Hungry?" Dad pushes a plate of pancakes toward me. He obviously doesn't see the creepy spirit.

"Uh…not really." I sit down slowly and watch the ghost follow Mom's every move. I'm so afraid I feel like I'm falling—my stomach drops and soars, twisting and forcing the bits of toothpaste I swallowed to crawl up my throat.

The ghost is an old, weathered man. His face is all wrinkles, and his eyes are black, squirming pits. He rises off the ground until he's hovering between the suspended metal rods hanging from the ceiling—the ones that hold Mom's pots and pans high in the air and out of the way.

"I know you can hear me, Elsie Edwards," the ghost says, its voice scratchy and raw. "Stay away from the Bone Tree… or else."

His voice makes me feel like one hundred steak knives just scratched across one hundred plates. Every centimeter of my skin is crawling.

The ghost shoves a heavy, cast iron pan off the rod.

"Watch out!" I shout at Mom.

She jumps out of the way just as the pan crashes onto the kitchen tile. "Holy smokes! How did that happen?" Mom fans herself with a dish towel.

"Good eye, Elsie. That could've been really bad." Dad pulls a chair over and investigates the rod.

The ghost is gone, but he leaves me with a serious case of the willies. This is not good—not one bit. I need to figure out what's going on at the Bone Tree.

"I'm going to go for a bike ride and maybe swing by Ashleigh's," I say abruptly.

Mom stops fanning herself and stares at me. "Seriously?"

"Yeah?" My stomach prickles with fear, but I ignore it. "Why?"

"We heard you crying last night, Elsie," Mom says. "I'm getting worried, kiddo. Would you be willing to talk to someone about Roman?"

I think, actually, I hope Roman is still floating around somewhere upstairs.

I pat Mom's arm and look between her and Dad. "I had a bad dream about Roman. That was it. I'm okay, guys, honest."

Mom and Dad let out equally long sighs, but they don't say anything else. They're very cautious around me, like I'm a cranky toddler seconds away from a face-melting tantrum.

"Okay, hon." Mom tosses me an apple. "Either call from Ashleigh's house or stop back here and let us know where you'll be. We might be going out later, so make sure you check in."

"Will do." I catch the apple and put it in my hoodie pocket. "See ya."

The shed is unlocked, so I grab my bike and pedal away with Roman floating beside me.

I fill him in on what happened in the kitchen.

"So what are we going to do now?" He asks, his pale face even paler than usual.

"We're going to the library," I say. "We need to know what we're dealing with."

—

We head out to the old, dusty library on Main Street. We stomp up the wooden stairs and push the heavy doors open. The library is built into a humongous, old house with shelves worming their way through the doorways. There are even shelves in the kitchen and bathrooms. There are no librarians around, so we pick the table farthest away from the front desk and wander through the bookstacks.

"What are we looking for?" Roman asks.

"We need to know more about the Bone Tree. If ghosts are forced to relive their deaths over and over to strengthen Mary, she must be really evil and strong by now. Maybe one of these books will tell us how to stop her."

"Okay, but you better get the books yourself, so we don't give the librarians a heart attack. And, you'll have to write things down when you want to talk to me unless you want to pretend you're crazy," Roman says.

"Roger that." I walk through the bookstacks until we have a stack of dusty books. When we get back, Ms. Young is at the front desk. I'm surprised. She's our school librarian. I didn't realize she worked here too. She loads books onto a cart and slowly pushes it down the aisle.

"Homework?" She peers at the old history books I'm holding as she walks by.

"A ton of it." I smile up at her.

Ms. Young polishes her glasses on her woolen dress. It has two kittens stitched into the front of it. Then she looks at me again, but it's like she's staring through me. "Okay then. Let me know if you two need anything."

My eyes triple in size. "What are you talking about?"

Roman's mouth falls open like a surprised goldfish.

Ms. Young hums off tune. "Nothing, dear."

I grab the first book and flop it open. I scan the index, but there isn't anything on the Bone Tree in this book. Or the next book. Or the book after that. After the fourth, I slam it shut and cross my arms. "What a waste of time."

"We can try googling it?" Roman whispers.

"We've already googled *it* a zillion times," I say.

"Is something the matter?" Ms. Young asks.

"No." I sigh.

Ms. Young is sitting at the table when I come back. She has a thermos open and two tiny cups full of steaming black liquid. "Sit down, child."

I sink into the chair across from her. I take a sip of the hot, sweet tea.

"You're not going to find anything about the Bone Tree in those books," Ms. Young says.

My mouth drops open. "How did you know that's what I was researching?"

"Someone looks into it every few years. Usually they're a lot older than you, but I suppose death doesn't pay attention to age." She smiles sadly in Roman's direction. "What do you want to know?"

I still can't figure out if she can see Roman or not. "What happens when you bury a token?"

"Well, you're getting right to it, aren't you?" Ms. Young clears her throat. "Once a token is buried, the token's owner is bound to the Bone Tree. Since their energy is no longer their own, they are in the care of whoever is linked to the tree. The only way to free the soul is to dig up the token."

So Grams would've been linked to Roman, but all of the other spirits are tied to Mary.

"I guess Samuel Simon skipped over that in his token pitch," I say.

Ms. Young chuckles. "I like to think he didn't know the pain he was causing. I do know that Mary is well aware, though she gives them another option. If they do what she asks, they won't be forced to endure unending death."

I try to keep my mouth from flopping over again. "You know about Mary?"

"Of course I do," Ms. Young says. "I gave her a token of my husband's."

Roman jumps up. "Holy crap!"

"You did?" I nearly choke on my tea. "Why?"

"I'm not sure if you've heard the stories around town, but Mary has a clever way of convincing people to bring her a token. When someone dies, she sends a ghost to their home.

If a child dies, she has the ghost of a little boy visit the grieving parents. He promises them they'll see their child if they bury a token."

"Did you see your husband?"

I can't believe old Ms. Young had a husband.

"Oh no," Ms. Young says. "Not at that moment, at least. No one ever sees who they're looking for. The only reason Mary is around is because her bones are buried. It appears you've found a loophole though. I don't tell people this, but I can sense spirits, including your friend over there. It's Roman, isn't it?"

Roman waves. "Hey, Ms. Young."

"Yeah, it's Roman. I buried his blood and hair at the Bone Tree. Why do you think Roman can leave the cemetery but Mary can't?" I feel rude asking so many questions, but I can't believe a grown-up knows about the Bone Tree.

"Oh child, Mary can leave. She has the strength from her tokens, but she just doesn't want to go anywhere." Ms. Young takes another sip of her tea. "What use would she have with the outside world, though? Roman leaves because he has a reason. He wants to see you. What I find strange is that Roman is functioning so well without a token."

"We think it's because I accidentally cut myself, and the Bone Tree sucked up some of my blood," I say.

"That's very interesting," Ms. Young says. "I've never heard of anyone tying their own energy to a spirit before."

"How do you know all of this stuff about the Bone Tree?" I ask. "Like about the ghosts dying and stuff."

"About a decade ago, I went to visit my husband's grave. I sensed that something was wrong with my sweet Seymour," Ms. Young says. "So I uncovered his token. I would've dug up the rest of them, but Mary showed up. I ran away as fast as I could. I haven't been back since. I suppose that makes me a bit of a coward, doesn't it?"

I shake my head.

"Well, that's enough talk for one morning." Ms. Young pulls herself to her feet and collects the thermos. "Be careful, Elsie…and you too, Roman."

I smile so hard my cheeks hurt. "We will. Thank you for your help."

Ms. Young winks at me and shuffles toward the front of the library.

"Wow." I turn and face Roman. "So there's an entire graveyard of people dying or enslaved just so one ghost doesn't have to cross over."

"I guess so," Roman says. He looks at me funny. "I know that look. You're thinking up a plan, aren't you?"

"I'm trying," I admit.

"Well, while you do that, I'm going to float into the attic," Roman says. "I've always wanted to know why they never let anyone up there. Try not to burn the place down with all your wheels turning."

I roll my eyes. Even as a ghost, Roman is the nosiest kid I know. I grab a pile of dusty books and carry them back to the shelves. I'm sliding them onto the shelf when I hear familiar voices echo through the aisles.

"The librarian said the self-help books were back here," Mrs. Pierce says.

"We don't need any books telling us how to raise our boy," Mr. Pierce growls.

"Well, whatever we're doing isn't working. Did you see his face? That is not the face of a boy who is accepting that his brother is gone," Mrs. Pierce says. Her voice is wobbling like she's about to burst into tears.

I peek through the books into their aisle. Mr. Pierce's face is scruffy and his eyes look heavy. Mrs. Pierce is buzzing around, resembling a bird trying to lift off the ground.

"Then we'll send him to the academy," Mr. Pierce says. "My dad sent me away after my mom died, and I turned out fine."

"We are not sending Jake to military school." Mrs. Pierce's eyes glaze over and her hands flap faster. She grabs a thick book off the shelf. A tearstained kid is on the front of it, along with the bold title of *Coping with Loss: A Guide to Sad Kids.*

I duck behind the next shelf of books before they can see me. The thought of Jake leaving makes my stomach hurt for some reason—maybe because he's Roman's brother.

"If they send me away, can I write you?" Jake asks from the table in front of me. I didn't even see him there.

"Sure, but I want real letters. Not emails." I plop down in the chair across from him and look up at the ceiling. The bottom of Roman's boots and jeans appear between the rafters. When Roman finally appears, I subtly nod my head back a few rows. Now is his shot to see his parents, no matter how sad they may be. "What are you doing here?" I ask Jake.

Roman waves frantically at his oblivious brother before floating over to his parents.

"My parents thought I needed to get out of the house. They're freaking out over nothing," Jake says.

I finally look at Jake and notice that *nothing* is definitely not *nothing*. "What happened?" I move to the seat next to Jake.

"Nothing," Jake says again, lowering his head.

I grab his chin and force him to face me. There's a dark purple bruise that shadows his cheekbone and disappears into his hair. "Did someone hit you?"

"Leave it alone, Elsie," Jake growls. His normally minty green eyes are dark and stormy, and I half expect a lightning bolt to shoot out and electrocute me.

"Not until you tell me what happened." I cross my arms and give him my best glare.

"My buddy said I was acting like a baby about Roman, so I knocked him out." Jake winces at the memory. "He got one in on me before he hit the ground."

Roman reappears and floats between us until Jake becomes a distorted blur. "Let's get out of here, Els. You were right. I shouldn't have come. My parents are talking about how sad everyone is, and it sucks."

I shoot Roman a look—a *Jake needs to talk to someone* look—but Roman doesn't catch it. Instead, Roman solidifies enough to grab my other arm and jerks me onto my feet.

"I want to go," he says. "Now!"

And then Roman vanishes, but this time it's on purpose.

Chapter 15

I CAN SMELL YOU

I LEAVE JAKE AND RUN OUT OF THE LIBRARY, BUT I'M too late—Roman is gone. I yank my bike out of the rack and climb on.

Maybe I will actually go to Ashleigh's like I told Mom I was going to.

I start to pedal, but my bike takes me away from Ashleigh's and toward the graveyard.

I think about turning around, but the thought that someone else's gram suffering under the tree keeps me going. When I get there, I ditch my bike near the short, iron fence and climb over it.

"Roman?" I whisper, in case he's nearby.

Squirrels chatter back, but Roman doesn't appear.

I walk down the path, slowing down as the Bone Tree comes into view. I look around, but there's no sign of Mary or any other ghosts. In the daytime, the tree is sort of pretty. The branches bow and sigh in the autumn breeze, leaves swirl and dance around the trunk, making the whole scene look like a nature ballet. Not that I've ever seen a ballet before. Without the pressure of resurrecting my best friend and scary ghost-witches, it's sort of peaceful.

I wander up to the tree and run my hands along the smooth trunk.

"How many souls do you have buried beneath your roots?" I murmur. I step over knots of raised roots and find the freshest hole. My stomach drops when I realize whose token is buried in the shallow grave.

"Oh no," I groan. I drop to my knees and frantically dig up a tiny, soft brown bear. Tears prickle my eyes as I clutch the bear to my chest. There's no way Mary could've used the little boy's energy. No ghost or monster could be that truly terrible.

A gentle breeze lifts my hair, and the smell of baby powder washes over me for a few seconds. I wonder if Theo's parents would've been able to see him if they bled on the tree as well?

"Rest in peace, Theo," I whisper. I shove the bear into my sweater pocket. There's no way I'm letting Mary get this one back—no matter what.

The breeze picks up again, but this time it turns into a howling wind. The temperature drops, along with my stomach. I dive behind a row of mostly-intact gravestones and lie flat on the ground. I pull clumps of broken branches overtop of me and pull my black hood over my hair. My heart is pounding so hard I have to check to make sure it's not making the dry leaves underneath me crackle.

Mary roars in with the blustering air. She soars upward, swirling and twisting through the branches of the Bone Tree.

"I know you're here, little girl," she screams. "I can smell you."

I press my fist into my mouth hard enough to taste blood.

Mary slithers up the trunk of the Bone Tree until she's hovering over the highest branch. She looks away from me and then slowly turns her head to the side, scanning the trees. Her head twists farther and farther until I can hear the *pop, pop* of her neck bones. The skin around her neck tears like wet paper. Black blood spills down her neck like ink as her head makes a full rotation.

Chunks of my breakfast slither up my throat, but I swallow them back down.

Voices echo from far away—most likely a family visiting a relative—so Mary swoops down and disappears into the brush.

I make sure the bear is still in my pocket before I jump up and dart down the path I took to get here. I'm running so fast I don't see the person in front of me until I run right into him.

"Oompf," Jake grunts. "Watch where you're going, kid."

"Hey, Jake, what are you doing here?" I ask. I look over my shoulder to make sure I'm alone.

"I was about to ask you the same thing." Jake looks past me and down the path. "Don't you know there are ghosts around here?"

"What?" I say, my eyes widen. What did Jake see? I open my mouth to try to explain when he cuts me off with a laugh.

"I'm just bugging ya." Jake bumps my shoulder with his fist. "Though there is a spooky old legend about this graveyard. Did Roman ever tell you the story about the tree back there?"

I shrug. "He mentioned it once or twice."

Jake steps over the fence. "Wanna go see it?"

"I can't, Jake. My mom will kill me if I'm late for dinner. Will you bike back with me? It's getting dark." I climb over the fence, so I'm no longer on the graveyard soil.

Jake grins at me and walks backward. "Sure, but you'll have to hang out here until I get back. I wanna see the Bone Tree."

"Wait." My legs feel like a zillion pounds, but I climb over the fence anyway. I can't let him go alone in case Mary comes back. "I'm coming."

I follow Jake down the path. The adrenaline sticking to my veins is the only thing keeping me from passing out. That and the fact that a demonic ghost-witch was here less than fifteen minutes ago. I need to start getting better sleep.

"You're quiet," Jake says. "When did that happen?"

Since your brother came back from the dead and ticked off an ancient spirit.

"I'm just tired," I say.

We come up to the Bone Tree. Thankfully, it's ghost-free.

Jake walks around the tree and slaps the trunk. "Too bad the old legend isn't true, hey?"

"Too bad," I echo.

"Okay, you're officially no fun," Jake says with a laugh. "Come on, Els. I'll bike back home with you and your lazy bones."

Jake steps over a root and directly into Theo's vacant hole. He topples over and lands in a heap.

"Are you okay?" I ask before I let myself laugh.

Jake pushes his hair out of his eyes and climbs to his feet. "Yeah, I'm fine."

I giggle, which is insanely unlike me, until I see blood trickle out from Jake's jacket. "You're bleeding!"

Jake shrugs his coat off and twists his arm, revealing a short, jagged cut. Blood trails down his arm like tiny, crimson rivers.

Roman falls from the sky, out of nowhere, and lands beside his brother. "Els, stop the bleeding. Use your sleeve or something."

"Nice of you to show up," I say under my breath. "He's fine."

"Elsie, the blood is dripping." Roman rushes forward, but his hands go right through Jake's arm.

I realize a second too late why Jake's bleeding is a bad thing. Before I can stop him, Jake wipes the blood off his arm and kneels down.

"Jake, no!" I lunge for his arm, but I'm not fast enough.

Jake smears his bloody hand over the dirt, and the ground sucks it up like a paper towel. "That was weird. Did you see that?"

Roman starts to flicker, like his body is being penetrated by pinpricks of light. "Uh-oh."

"Roman?" Jake falls onto his butt and crabwalks backward into the tree.

And then the Bone Tree and its magic makes Roman disappear. Again.

Chapter 16

BLACK PITS

IT'S HARD ENOUGH RUNNING THROUGH THE WOODS WHEN it's dark. It's even harder chasing someone who's a full foot taller than you.

"Jake, wait!" I hold my arms out in front of me to keep the twigs from whipping my face.

Jake doesn't stop running until we're outside of the main gate. When I catch up to him, he's so mad his face is red.

"Why didn't you tell me?" He roars.

"I can explain," I pant.

"I bawled like a baby at his grave, and you just let me." Jake slumps against the huge iron gate. "You let me cry even though he was here, all along."

An icy breeze tickles the back of my neck, and my gut screams at me to run. "Jake, we need to get out of here. Now."

Jake is quiet for a minute. He looks between his bike and the graveyard before he shakes his head. "No, we need to go back to the Bone Tree. I need to see Roman. I need to see if he's really back." Jake pushes past me and heads for the fence.

I grab Jake's shoulder. "Listen to me for a second. Roman isn't there. When the Bone Tree got your blood, something weird happened to Roman. He'll find us, but we need to get out of here."

"Not a chance." Jake turns around before I can stop him and sprints around the tree. "Roman! Roman!"

An unearthly howl bellows from somewhere in the woods.

Jake pauses and looks at me.

"I'll explain everything…but we need to go. Now," I say.

Thankfully, Jake agrees. We take off down the path as fingers of branches reach for our sleeves. We take off before Mary, the little soul snatcher, can spot us. Neither of us makes a peep until we make it back to my house. I run up the sidewalk and stop to catch my breath.

I fumble in my pocket for my house keys—Mom and Dad are freaks about locking the doors even if they're home–but when I look up, Jake is gone.

—

I can't sleep. I think about how Mary could be float-ing outside my window. I can't risk opening my window to

check. Then I change my mind, I have to know. I slide out
of bed and tiptoe to the window. I press my face against
the glass and peer into the backyard, but all I see is the
twisted shadows of my normal, non-magical, non-haunted
tree. When I look up again, Mary is hanging upside down
in front of my window. I stifle a scream and jerk back. I
wait for her to float inside, but she doesn't. I jump back into
bed, pull the blankets up to my eyeballs and push my back
against the wall farthest from the window.

Mary is watching me right now.

Her hair is floating around her head as if she's underwa-
ter. Her skin is moldy and gray. Her eyes are black pits.

She's not real. You're just tired. Go to sleep.

I close my eyes for a second, but I can't keep them closed.
I need to see if she's watching me. I open my eyes. She's still
outside, but this time she's smiling. I yank my comforter off
the bed, wrap it around myself and race into the hallway.
I creep down the stairs and into my dad's office—the only
room without a window. I curl up on the cracked leather
couch and close my eyes. I'm so exhausted I fall asleep.

When I open my eyes, the clock in my dad's office reads
3:16 a.m.

*Shoot, I better get up before Mom and Dad find me here. But
better than Mary finding me.* I drag myself off the couch and
quietly back upstairs to my room. Mary is gone when I go
back into my room, but I can't go back to sleep. Roman still
hasn't shown up, but it's okay. I need to talk to Jake before
Roman makes his grand entrance.

I stay awake, back pressed against the wall, my eyes on the window until the sun comes up. The second I hear Mom's alarm, I quickly get dressed and yell out some excuse about going to Ashleigh's. I grab my bike and ride the empty streets toward Jake and Roman's house. It's early enough that there isn't anyone else on the road. As I turn into the Pierce's neighborhood, a shadow flickers in the corner of my eye. I think it's a bird, but when I turn to see, there isn't anything there.

I pedal faster. The wind picks up and whooshes into my ears. It almost sounds like a voice.

"Elssssie," the wind hisses.

"Stay away from me!" I scream and pedal as fast as I can, even though I know I can't out run the air itself. The wind is ice cold and stings my face. I wince and swivel my head around, expecting to see Mary, but no one is on the street but me.

"Stay away," a voice says in the icy wind.

I jump the curb and leap off my bike. I sprint into the Pierce's backyard and slam the gate behind me. Mary is gone, for now at least. The back door is unlocked, so I run right in. I knock on Jake's closed door and slide down onto my butt in front of it. I cover my face with my hands and try to stop panting.

"Mom?" Jake asks from behind his bedroom door.

"No, it's me. I'm sorry." I rest my head against his door. I take another gasping breath and listen for his parents. The upstairs is silent. "I wasn't trying to keep Roman away from you, but what was I supposed to say? 'Hey Jake, I used the Bone Tree to bring your brother back.' "

"That's pretty much exactly what you should have said." Jake must have shuffled over to my side of the door because I can hear him like he's speaking right into my ear. "I would've believed you."

I lean my head back, so it thumps against the hollow wood. "No, you wouldn't have. Not even if we told you our plan before Roman died. It was his idea, by the way. He gave me his hair and blood to bury…that's why the Bone Tree doesn't work for anyone else. Part of you needs to be buried under it to work. Anyways, everything is different now. The Bone Tree is using our blood—our life force or whatever—to give Roman energy. He's not a normal ghost now. No one else will be able to see or hear him but us."

"I know the story, Els," Jake says. "What if my parents went to the actual tree? What if they bled on it? Would they be able to see Roman?"

"I'm being haunted," I say quietly. "What if that happens to them?"

Jake is quiet for so long I think he may have fallen asleep. I get up to leave but stop when his door cracks open. He walks out, his face stained with fresh tears and grabs onto my sleeve. "Where did Roman go? I saw him for a few seconds, and then he disappeared."

I look down at his hand tangled in my sweatshirt. "When the Bone Tree took my blood, he left for a while. He should come back soon. Don't worry."

Jake lets out a long, shaky breath. "I didn't think I'd ever see him again."

"Me neither."

Silence takes over again, along with the weird realization that I'm alone with Jake.

"I should go home." I pull my arm away from Jake and turn away. "I'll let you know when Roman shows up."

Jake runs around me and blocks the door. "Don't leave, Els."

Els?

Something in the living room behind us makes the floor creak.

"Don't let me interrupt." Roman flops onto the couch and picks up the remote. He clicks on the TV and channel surfs as Jake and I stare at him. He looks so normal it's a little unsettling. His cheeks are flushed, his eyes the same bright blue, the only thing that resembles the sick boy who left us forty-one sleepless nights ago is his bony shoulders.

"Roman?" Jake pushes his fist against his mouth.

"Hey, big brother." Roman climbs off the couch, and they both do the weird approach all guys do when they're about to hug.

Jake moves first and scoops his brother up in a back-breaking hug. He buries his face in the shoulder of Roman's hoodie, and I can tell by his shaking shoulders that he's crying again.

Roman thumps Jake on the back. "I missed you too."

They break apart a minute later, both of them with huge smiles on their faces. We sit on the floor in a triangle.

Jake won't stop staring at Roman. "I can't believe you're here."

Roman grins. "You have Els to thank for that."

Jake turns his megawatt smile on me, and my stomach tumbles like Iron Man falling out of the sky. "Thanks," he says.

I will my cheeks to stay a normal color. Now is most definitely not the time to crush on Jake—no matter how perfect his smile is. "No problem."

"So now what?" Jake asks.

"Before you showed up, I helped a ghost cross over. At least I think I did. Do you remember that couple that buried the teddy bear out at the tree, Roman?" I say.

He nods.

"I dug up the teddy bear so Mary couldn't use the energy. I smelled baby powder when I pulled the bear out of the hole . . .I think I set him free. If I did, that means there are tons of ghosts still bound to the Bone Tree. They're stuck reliving their own deaths over and over again, just like Grams, while Mary uses up all the lingering energy left in their tokens."

"Who's Mary?" Jake asks.

Roman fills Jake in on Mary and all the souls in-between. I perch on the edge of the couch and stare out the window.

"Uh, I have to tell you guys something," I say. "Mary was floating outside my window all night last night."

"Well, I'm not leaving your side," Roman says. "Ever again."

I grin at Roman. "So what do we do about all the other souls?"

"We can't leave their tokens there. You saw your Grams, Els. All those tokens are people's grandmothers or kids or whatever. They deserve to be free," Roman says.

The thought of going back to the graveyard makes me shiver.

"Jake and I will do it though. I'm not going to risk Mary getting her hands on you," Roman says.

I snort. "I'm coming with you guys. Don't bother telling me no because I'll just sneak out and come anyway."

Roman and Jake let out identical sighs.

"Don't even," I snap. "I've only crossed over a couple of spirits so far. There could be hundreds surrounding the tree—dying over and over again. You need my help, and I'm coming. End. Of. Story."

Roman and Jake exchange glances.

"We're going tonight," Jake says.

I smile, my stomach twisting into knots. I nod at the brothers. "Tonight."

Chapter 17

FREE ALL THE GHOSTS

UNFORTUNATELY, JAKE AND I STILL NEED TO GO TO SCHOOL. So once I'm done at the Pierce's, I pedal home and sneak back into my room. It's already nighttime. The day flew by with Jake and Roman. The clock glows 11:30 p.m. I groan, change into my jammies and get not enough sleep before Mom knocks on my door.

"Rise and shine, kiddo!" She sings. She flings my drapes open and a sunbeam laser hits my eyes.

My eyes feel like sandpaper. I need to sleep more if I'm going to be any kind of help tonight at the Bone Tree. I let out a weak cough.

"Ma, I'm sick," I say pathetically.

She snorts. "Yeah, right. I heard you shuffling around your room in the middle of the night, , young lady. If you can stay up until God knows when in the morning, you can go to school"

My blood turns to cherry Slurpee in my veins. What was she talking about? I was asleep by 11:30 p.m. I wasn't walking around my room in the wee hours of the morning. Mary must've been walking around my room while I was asleep. The thought of her lurking while I was asleep makes me want to bawl my eyes out.

"I'll make pancakes," Mom continues, completely oblivious to my terror. "Now get up and shower, my little ray of sunshine."

"I'll make pancakes," Mom continues, completely oblivious to my terror. "Now get up and shower, my little ray of sunshine."

—

School is finally back to normal. No one stops me to talk about Roman—no one except Claire that is. My teachers stop skipping over me when it comes time to read out loud. Ashleigh, Levi, and Carlee even pretend like I haven't been ditching them every second.

"Hey, wanna come over and play ping-pong after school?" Levi asks between second and third period.

"Sure," I say, and for the first time since Roman got sick, I actually mean it.

His face lights up. "Awesome! I'll text my mom, so she makes that nacho dip you like."

"Sweet," I say with a grin.

Roman drifts down the hall toward me. "Are we going to the Dawson's after school?"

"We sure are," I mutter under my breath. The last thing I need is for people to think I'm talking to myself once they start acting normal around me again.

"Cool," he says. "I'm going to go hang out in the teacher's lounge and see what they chat about. I'll find ya later."

Roman disappears into the wall, and I turn into my math class. I take my usual seat near the back—I stink at math—and doodle on my notebook as the rest of the kids trickle in.

A cool breeze ripples over my arms, and I shiver. Why would they have the air conditioning on in the fall? I look up and realize it's not the AC—it's a ghost.

A girl wearing high-waisted pants that flare out into giant bell-bottoms stands in front of one of the second story windows. She yanks the window open and leans out of it. Her skin glows orange from an invisible fire before her exposed stomach starts to blister. She swings one leg out the window, her mouth yawning in a silent scream. Her pants catch on fire and then *whoosh,* she tumbles out the open window. I stare, my mouth hanging open until she appears in front of me again. The whole horrible scene replays again and again until I can't take it anymore.

I jerk out of my desk and grab my backpack. "I need to use the bathroom."

I rush out of the room before my teacher has a chance to say anything. I run down the halls looking for Roman and end up outside of the library. I duck inside and pray there aren't any ghosts in here.

"I believe," Ms. Young says from her big, cluttered desk,

"that you have some explaining to do."

I cover my eyes with my hands. "Please don't tell me they're in here too."

Ms. Young clucks her tongue. "Only a hanging man but don't worry, he tends to stay between the bookstacks. Now come back here and sit down. You're as white as a…well… as a ghost."

I shuffle behind the desk and move some books off a little footstool. I sink and let out a long, shaky breath. "This is my fault. I took another spirit from Mary, and she's angry."

Ms. Young pulls out her trusty thermos and pours me a tiny cup of tea. "What is your plan, Elsie?"

I shrug helplessly. "I want to free all of the ghosts."

"And what about Mary?" She asks.

"Well, if all the tormented spirits are free, Mary shouldn't be evil…right?" I take a sip of my tea.

"In theory." Ms. Young hums. "But having the kind of power that she does could be addicting. She could start collecting tokens again, and then what?"

"Then I'll dig them up again," I say.

"You'll spend your whole life playing cat and mouse with Mary so you can keep Roman around?"

"It's not just that. I need to save those souls." I'm not lying about saving the souls, but keeping Roman around is essential. I've had a taste of life without my best friend, and I don't want to try it ever again.

"It might not always be as easy as digging up a locket, Elsie," Ms. Young says quietly. "Don't underestimate Mary and her own hunger for life."

"I won't," I say. I finish my tea and hand her the cup. "I guess I better get back to class."

"One moment," she says, reaching back into the narrow drawer. "Sprinkle this in your classroom. It won't get rid of the ghosts for good, but it should at least keep them out of your line of vision."

She presses a saltshaker into my hand. "But bring that back. Hard-boiled eggs without salt is a sin."

I take the salt and put it in my pocket. "Thanks, Ms. Young. For everything."

She squeezes my hand, leaving smudges of ink behind. "Be careful, Elsie."

"I will," I say.

At least, I'll try.

Chapter 18
THE TOKENS

THE SALT KEEPS THE GHOSTS AWAY ENOUGH SO I CAN make it through the rest of the day. Even though I'm exhausted from last night, I still go to game night at the Dawson's. Thankfully, their house is ghost-free, other than Roman. I guess that's a perk of living in a new neighborhood—no one has died in their house.

Right before Roman and I leave, Ashleigh throws her arms around me and squeezes me tight.

"It was fun hanging out with you," she says. "It's been way too long."

"I know," I say. "I'm still dealing with some stuff."

She nods. "My birthday party is next week. My mom is taking us to that new amusement park a few hours away. Do you wanna come?"

I look at Roman. There's no way he'll be able to be that

far away from the Bone Tree, and there's no way I can be that far from Roman.

I shake my head. "My parents are kinda clingy these days, so I don't think they'll let me go. I'm really sorry. I'll make it up to you, I swear."

"Oh, okay, that's fine," she says. "We'll do something else. Maybe we can go to the park here instead?"

I give her a huge smile. "That'd be great. Tell the twins I say thanks again. I'll see you at school, kay?"

"Kay," she says. She smiles, but it doesn't seem like a real one.

"You can go out of town, ya know," Roman says as she shuts the door.

"I don't know how long you're going to be here for," I say. "I'm not missing one minute with you, even for a roller coaster."

Roman doesn't say much on the walk home.

When we get back to my place, I fill my parents in on my day and crash hard. I'm pretty sure I'm still snoring when Roman wakes me up a few hours later.

"Els," he whispers in my ear. His cold breath washes over my cheek and sends a shock of chills down my spine. "Do you want me to go without you? Jake and I can handle things tonight." I look at the clock, it's eleven o'clock.

I've never wanted to say *yes* so badly in my life, but I can't let them do this alone. Whether they'll admit it or not, they need me.

"I'm coming." I groan and stuff some gum in my mouth, even though I doubt I slept long enough to get morning breath.

I climb out of the window and leap onto the trampoline. My knees buckle instantly, and I clumsily roll off the black nylon. Roman drifts gracefully to the ground like a falling leaf.

"Let's go," I whisper. I grab my bike out of the shed and sneak out of the backyard.

—

When we reach the graveyard, Jake is already waiting for us near the black fence.

"Hey," he says. "I wasn't sure if you were going to show up."

I roll my eyes.

He nudges me with his shoulder. "What's the plan then?"

"I'll tell you on the way," I say. I just want to get this over with. I know that I want to help as many ghosts as I can, but I also know that if I don't get some sleep, some normal sleep, I'm going to turn into a ghost myself.

We walk in silence down the now familiar path toward the Bone Tree. Roman zooms ahead to make sure the coast is clear. As Jake and I get closer, fog starts to swirl around our feet, growing thicker with each step.

"This can't be good," Jake mutters.

The fog billows up, separating into humanlike shapes. The pillar of mist closest to me starts writhing. It's a woman—a young one—with wet hair and clothes. She screams silently, water pouring out of her mouth, her eyes bulging out of her head. She windmills her arms, but she doesn't go anywhere. And then suddenly—she stops. Her arms float eerily above her head like she's sinking into the sea. And then she appears to drown, again.

"Oh my gosh," I whisper as more and more ghosts take form.

"Are they...dying?" Jake asks. His face is pale, and beads of sweat are starting to roll down his forehead.

I nod and reach for his arm. I grab hold of his sweatshirt and pull him through the swarms of twitching, vomiting, wailing ghosts. It feels good to be the brave one.

We make it to the tree, and I grab Jake's backpack off of his shoulder. I unzip it and pull out a couple of gardening shovels.

"I think we should dig holes until we find a bunch of tokens, and then pull them out as fast as we can," I say. I dig into my back pockets and pull out a few crumpled plastic bags. "Jake, make sure you keep all the tokens with you. If we leave any behind, Mary will just bury them again. Roman, do you want to keep an eye out for Mary?"

"You got it." Roman salutes and then drifts back into the trees.

Jake and I crawl around the Bone Tree, pushing our shovels into the dry earth, scooping out shovelfuls into small piles.

Something slides out of my pocket and lands with a metallic clang, but I don't have time to stop and look for it now. It's probably just a few quarters or something.

I mark each uncovered token with a broken twig, so I don't lose track of any. If we pull them out as we go, we won't finish before Mary shows up, and I do not want to be here when she realizes what we're up to.

Ghosts begin to split up and hover near their tokens.

"Release me," an old, withered man begs as he tumbles forward, somersaulting through the dirt before his neck snaps viciously to the side. He vanishes, reappearing near an old, silver pocket watch that is lying in the dirt.

"Let's do this," I say. I grab the pocket watch out of the hole. Just then, a huge man approaches me. Before he reaches me, his left leg blows off, and he falls backward landing next to a rusted set of dog tags. Before he can begin the process again, I shove the dog tags into my bag and reach for the next token.

Jake and I move as fast as we can, grabbing tokens and watching spirits disappear before moving onto the next.

When we finish, I tie the bag shut and loop it around my wrist.

"That was…easy," I pant. "It was too easy."

"Have you seen Roman?" Jake asks.

The forest around us is so eerily silent that I can hear the critters scurrying around the leaves at my feet.

"Not since we started," I say. "Roman?"

Jake dares to yell, "Roman!"

I look up, but I can't see Roman anywhere. Then a tiny, weak Roman-sounding cough comes from somewhere behind the Bone Tree. Before we can run to him, the trees start to shake. Mary bursts through the branches, but this time she doesn't look like much of a ghost. She has brown, curly hair that hangs down her shoulders. Her skin is pale, her eyes wide and dark.

This is what she must've looked like when she was alive.

When she looks down, the transformation begins. Her hair mattes into clumps and chunks of it fall out. Her skin decomposes and turns a funky, greenish-gray. Her nails grow and twist into black talons—her eyes become soulless, black holes. I grab Jake, but now it's too late to run.

It's too late to do anything but scream.

Chapter 19

LET THEM GO

I REACH FOR JAKE BUT SHOUT FOR HIS BROTHER. "ROMAN!"

Jake and I scramble to the other side of the Bone Tree where Roman is lying helpless, but Mary throws a wall of dirt up between us before we can reach him. The flying pieces of earth blur my sight of Roman's now heaving body. I once read that old ghosts are more powerful, but I didn't think she'd be like this. I didn't think she'd be so powerful. I let go of Jake and run through the dirt, ignoring the sting of tiny sticks.

"Mary somehow buried a token of mine. You have to get out of here." Roman gasps. He's back to nothing but mist, but he looks worse than he did before. He's so skinny again with black smears under his eyes. His hair is patchy and black strands litter the shoulders of his red sweatshirt. He closes his eyes, and a racketing, shuttering breath fills the air. Then he's lifeless. In one terrifying moment, I lose my best friend all over again.

"Roman!" I grab his sweatshirt, but my hands go right through him. "Come back!"

Mary circles around the tree, her fingers fly as she counts the ghosts still bound to the tree that we can't see. Her skin is gray and saggy, hanging off her cheekbones like old curtains. She whips her arms around, making the wind twirl around at hurricane speeds. She screams at the ghosts, "Bring her to me!"

Sweat pours down my forehead and my stomach cramps. I'm going to die, and then Jake is going to die. Roman writhes on the ground before he goes motionless again. He's going to be stuck like this forever if I don't do something.

"What do you want with me?" I dig my heels into the ground as swarms of ghosts push me toward Mary.

"I know what your blood did for your little friend," Mary hisses. "I'm going to bleed you dry."

"I don't care what you do to me," I spit out. "But dig up Roman's token. Let him go free. If you do that, I'll let you do whatever you want."

Roman wheezes and shakes again. This is the second time he's relived his death. I realize now that his parents are liars. They told me he died peacefully—they lied.

There's nothing peaceful about this. No wonder Mary wants the tokens. She doesn't want to die again.

Mary tips her head back and howls with laughter. She sounds like a werewolf in one of those old black and white horror movies. "I don't need to bargain with you, child. I already have you and your friends. I can do whatever I want to them once your blood has been spilled."

"Please let them go," I beg. "Please."

Mary floats down so her face is hovering in front of mine. "Time to die, little one."

"Not if I can help it." Jake chucks a handful of open salt packages at Mary—something straight out of the *How to Kill Spirits Playbook*.

Mary screeches and flies backward into the trees.

Jake and I make it to Roman just in time for him to wake up again.

"How do we move him?" I plunge my fingers into Roman's shoulders, and they crunch into the cold ground below.

"You don't," Roman wheezes. "Run. I'll find a way to get to you."

"We can't leave him!" I shout above Mary's wails.

A horrible, scratching fills the air. It's so grating every single hair on my body turns into a pin that stabs me over and over. I whip around just as Mary smashes broken gravestones together into a giant concrete ball. It rises off the ground, hypnotically swaying in the howling wind until it's brushing against the highest branches of the Bone Tree.

"Jake," Roman gasps. "Get out of here. Now."

Jake hesitates for a second before he grabs my wrist and hauls me to my feet. I wrench my wrist free, but he just grabs my other one. "We'll come back for him, I promise."

The remaining leaves on the trees above rain down on us as the chunks of marble and stone rise higher and higher.

"Where are you, little girl?" Mary soars into the air, her arms held high above her head, and scans the ground.

"Run!" Jake tugs me toward my usual path, and this time I listen. Branches snap and crash behind us as the gigantic rock hurls through the air, no longer held up by Mary's death magic. I turn around mid-run and trip over a root, taking Jake down with me. My chin bounces off a rock, and I nip the tip of my tongue with my teeth. My tongue throbs and I taste blood, but it gives me an extra boost of energy. Jake hauls me up to my feet, and we clear out just in time for the rock to smash to the ground.

"Go left!" I bodycheck Jake into the trees and leap after him. The rock shatters, spitting out chunks of tombstones as it cartwheels past us.

Mary's howls grow louder as we push our way through the dense trees and hurl ourselves over the fence. We grab our bikes before we speed off into the night, only stopping to open my back gate and pedal into the dark backyard.

—

"We'll go back for Roman in a minute. I just need to fix my face." I spit out a mouthful of blood and grab the lowest hanging branch on the tree that leads into my bedroom window. I pull myself up, my arms shaking like the leaves and wait for Jake.

"You go up first," he says. "I'll climb behind you in case you fall."

I normally would reply with a snarky comment, but I'm just too tired. Besides, falling out of my own tree isn't out of the question. I wait halfway through the window for Jake to make it onto the roof. Once he's safely inside, I lock the window to my bedroom and collapse onto my comforter. Part of me wants to wake my parents up and tell them the whole thing. The other part knows they'll think I'm crazy. Or they'll be so ticked off I snuck out that they'll lock me in my room forever. I can't risk it. I need to get back to Roman.

Jake passes me a cup of day-old water off of my nightstand. "You should rinse the blood out of your mouth."

I swish the water around my mouth and swallow with disgust. I fall back down on my bed and drop my head between my knees. "I think we should rest for a few minutes and then go back for Roman."

Jake sits down and shakes his head. "We can't go back for him, Elsie."

"But he's your brother." I try to sit up, but my head swirls. "We can't just leave him there."

Jake pulls a twig out of his hair and looks me in the eye. I realize I haven't even asked if *he* was okay. I quickly look him over, and aside from a couple dozen tiny scratches crisscrossing over his cheeks and forehead, he seems fine. "We'll save him, okay? But first we need to come up with a plan. We can't just walk into the cemetery anymore—it's too dangerous. Mary isn't going to leave the Bone Tree now," Jake says.

"We can take her."

Jake laughs softly. "Maybe, yeah, but I don't want to risk it tonight. I don't want to get Roman in any more trouble."

One of my parents, probably Dad, gets out of bed and walks softly down the hall toward the kitchen. I hold my breath and wait for his sixth sense to kick in. Neither of us speaks a word until the hallway is silent again.

Jake stands up and winces as he puts weight on his knee. "Speaking of trouble, I better go before your parents catch me in here."

I grab his hand before he can reach my window. "I know I'm being a baby, but can you stay here until I fall asleep?"

He has a look in his eyes that I can't figure out. "Sure."

I let go of his hand and pull the blankets up under my chin. "Thanks."

Jake sits on the corner of my bed and rests his back against the wall. He slips off his shoes, careful to keep the dirty bottoms from touching my quilt and crosses his arms over his chest.

"There's a blankie under your butt," I mumble sleepily.

"A blankie, huh?" Jake shifts on the bed and tugs free the large blanket Grams knitted for me. "I'll let that one slide because you're so tired."

I pull the blanket up, and each time I move, pieces of dirt fall off of my face and onto my pillowcase. Dried leaves crumble off my clothes and grind into my sheets. I'm definitely going to have to change these sheets in the morning, or Mom is going to have some serious questions.

Even though I can't sleep right away, Jake and I don't talk. Maybe it's because we're afraid to admit that neither one of us has a plan on how to get Roman back.

After twenty long minutes, I roll onto my side and bury my face in my pillow.

"Night, Jake."

"Night, Els."

—

I wake up to the whisper of metal sliding against metal. Jake is gone, my lamp is turned off and my room is filled with shadows. I sit up and listen for the noise again, even though it's probably just Dad getting up for a drink.

Sccccratch.

That is definitely not Dad. I pull the blankets up to my eyeballs and scan my room. It looks empty, but that doesn't mean it is.

Sccccratch.

The sound is coming from inside my closet. I wish I hadn't left the door open. I squint and stare into the darkness, but there isn't any sign of Mary. A shadow flutters from somewhere deep in the racks of T-shirts and summer clothes.

I stuff my blanket against my mouth to keep from screaming. Then slowly, so slowly, a wire hanger slides against the hanging metal rod.

Sccccratch.

Chapter 20

THE SHACK

I TOSS AND TURN ALL NIGHT, NEVER COMING OUT FROM UNDER my blankets, but I force myself out of bed as soon as I hear Dad lazily drag himself down the hallway. I investigate my closet—braver now that the sun is shining—but whatever was in there is gone. I check myself out in my wall mirror and cringe. My entire chin is covered in a black and purple bruise.

Thankfully, Mom bought me some makeup for my birthday, so I use a bit of the skin-colored goop to cover it. I twist my hair into a braid, pull on my favorite jeans and push my ripped sweatshirt as far down the hamper as it'll go. I put on a long-sleeved T-shirt, my lucky socks and psyche myself up to face Mary and save my best friend.

Jake left me a note telling me to meet him at our usual spot at the graveyard fence. I spin Mom and Dad a lie about extra homework and movie night at the Dawson's. It's auction day—the one day a month Mom and Dad take off to bargain hunt with or without me—so they won't even notice if I'm gone all day. They leave before I do, already chatting about the good deals.

Jake is pacing in front of the iron l fence when I get there.

"Hey," he says. "What took you so long?"

"Your note didn't say a time, dummy," I say. I'm so antsy I want to leap out of my skin. "What's the plan?"

"Do you remember when our old teacher got sick, and Ms. Young took over for the week for all grades?" Jake asks.

I nod. "I'm pretty sure everyone remembers those few weeks. Why?"

Jake takes off along the fence and back toward the part of the old cemetery that no one visits anymore—except maybe Mary. He crunches through leaves, his breath coming out in slightly frosty puffs.

"Well, she was the one who first told me about the Bone Tree. She knew all about Fredric Falls and the town legends. I think she even wrote a history book on Samuel and Mary," Jake says.

Really? She never mentioned that to me.

"Get to the point!" I shout. "Sorry, I just can't stop thinking about Roman."

"I know," Jake says. "Me too, but this will help. I think. Ms. Young told us this other story…one about these tunnels. Fredric Falls was a hot spot during Prohibition. There were makeshift distilleries hidden all throughout the forest where they made illegal booze. To transport it to different areas, they dug a series of tunnels underneath the town."

"So how does that help us?" I ask.

"It made me remember an old episode of *Ghost Adventures*. Something about ghosts not being able to go underneath the ground at their burial sites…" Jake trails off.

"Oh my gosh!" I grab Jake's arm and excitedly yank it. "You're a genius."

Jake smirks. "Now all we have to do is find a way to get into one of those tunnels. Since they were dug in the 1920s, the entrances are probably going to be in some really old buildings."

I rack my brain for where Jake may be leading us. "The old gatekeeper shack?" I ask.

"Yeah, that might be the best place to start. That and I already checked town hall and the old library before I came here," Jake says.

My mouth drops open. "Seriously?"

Jake rolls his eyes a little. "Don't act so surprised. Roman is your best friend, but he's my brother."

Yeah, he may have a point there.

—

The ancient, wooden gatekeeper shack is up ahead. Mom said they had a problem with grave robbers back in the day, so the cemetery was always locked. When it expanded, the town couldn't afford to build tall fences, so they put the short iron ones in and got rid of the gate, hoping that grave robbing was something of the past.

Jake reaches the shack first and tries the door. When the old thing doesn't budge, he gives it a few decent shoulder checks before it explodes inward.

I make a mental note to donate my allowance to the town's heritage fund to fix the door and follow him inside. The shack is dank and gloomy, and it smells like old leaves and cat pee. It's empty aside from a small wooden table and one single chair. There's a square, wooden hatch built into the floor.

"Oh great," I say. "The entrance is going to be in the cellar, isn't it?"

Jake wrinkles his nose. "Most likely."

I shoot him a look. "Afraid of spiders or something?"

Jake glares at me. "Don't act like you aren't."

I ignore him, grab the hatch and yank it open. A mushroom cloud of dust explodes up and into my face, but thankfully there aren't any ghosts. Not yet anyway.

Jake uses his cell phone flashlight to light the way as I carefully crawl down the short ladder and into the cellar. It's so small that Jake has to hunch over to walk.

A small wooden door is built into the far wall. A couple of lanterns rest on a barrel that still smells a bit like alcohol, even after all these years. Unfortunately, we don't have a map, so we have no idea where this tunnel will lead us.

I push the door open, and it swings into the tunnel. Spider webs hang in the opening, and I swear I hear the skittering of tiny little insect legs.

Sparks of fire light up the room as Jake lights the old glass lanterns. "Here, take one."

"Thanks." I accept a glowing lantern from Jake and follow him into the tunnel.

"Stick close to me," he says. "I don't want either of us getting lost."

The tunnel is high enough that I can walk standing up straight, but Jake has to duck under the wooden support beams every ten feet or so. It's not too bad at first, but once we turn the first corner, the lingering cellar light is swallowed up by the blackest darkness I've ever seen.

I keep my eyes glued to the path in front of me. Every once in a while, we come across a glass bottle or two—probably from someone sampling the alcohol while hustling the booze through the tunnels. The walls are all dirt except for the wooden arches every few feet. Spiders and centipedes scurry away from the light. I pull my sleeves over my hands in case any of them take a flying leap at me. I can handle ghosts, but bugs are a no-go.

We keep walking until the tunnel comes to a fork. Jake puts down his lantern and launches the compass app on his phone. "The Bone Tree is in the northeast corner of the cemetery. If we head in that direction, we could find another exit."

"Why would there be an exit there?" I ask. I try to stop myself from shivering, but I can't. I shake so hard my teeth chatter. Dad would say it's the kind of cold that makes your bones ache. But the tunnel isn't just a cold that makes your bones ache—it's bone-chilling terrifyingly cold.

"Before the care of the cemetery got taken over by a city company, Mary and Samuel Simon's kids and then their kids took care of it. I bet you any money they agreed to have a tunnel exit in the graveyard. What better place for it to come up than near the Bone Tree? Maybe they could convince a few of the local businessmen to bury a token or two for Mary," Jake says.

"Wow," I say. "Someone has been doing their homework."

"I couldn't sleep last night, so I did some research," Jake says. "Like I said, he's my brother. I'll do whatever it takes to save him, even if it does mean I have to read outside of class."

We walk in silence until Jake hits his head on a gnarled, white tree root. He grunts and looks up. "I think this is it."

"Could you help me?" I point at the ground above our heads. We need to get the tokens from beneath the Bone Tree—no matter what.

Jake growls but drops to his knees. I climb shakily onto his back and stand up. I scratch at the packed clay and dirt overhead, making bits and pieces of it rain down on Jake's neck. He shakes it off, almost bucking me off in the process.

"It's dirt," I whisper. "Not bugs. Chill."

I rake my fingers against the dirt ceiling until every single one of my nails breaks. I can't find a single thing. I climb off Jake and fall onto my butt, blinking to keep from crying, but the tears come anyway. "This is stupid. I don't even know what I'm looking for."

Jake sits next to me. The mini cavern is glowing with the lantern light, and for one small second, I forget how scared I am.

"Let's think for a minute," Jake says. "What could Mary have used as a token? I wasn't wearing any of Roman's clothes, and Mary hasn't taken anything from his room. Not that she could…Mom doesn't really ever leave it."

Then it hits me. "I lost my keys." I squeeze Jake's hand with my dirty one.

"Els, this isn't really the time to think about where you left your keys—"

"No, Jake, listen for a second. I lost them the last time we were at the Bone Tree. I was super bummed because Roman gave me his Thor keychain before he died. They must have fallen out of my pocket into the dirt when we were digging up the tokens to free the ghosts."

Jake drops onto all fours again. "Well climb on and get looking then."

I ignore my aching fingers and claw at the packed dirt like a dog digging up his buried bones until I finally hit metal.

"I found them!" I pick and pinch them until I finally yank them down from the dirt. I press a kiss into Thor's dirty head before jamming my keys into my pocket. "I'm never losing these again."

I jump off of Jake's back and search for Roman. Now that I have his token, he must be strong again. But he doesn't show up. We wait for what feels like an eternity, but it's probably only a few minutes until Roman suddenly appears in between Jake and me. He's back to normal, well as normal as Bone-Tree Roman can look. He holds out his arms, and I launch myself into them.

"I'm so sorry we left you." I squeeze him tight and ignore his iciness.

"I'm so happy Jake made you leave." Roman lets me go and fist bumps his brother. "You two would've been goners if you stayed. Mary's so ticked off there isn't a tombstone for miles that's not in pieces."

"What took you so long?" I blurt out.

"I felt myself going back to normal, but I couldn't just stand up and walk away. Mary hasn't left the Bone Tree since you guys escaped. She spent all night watching me die...over and over again." Roman looks up at the gnarled roots of the Bone Tree. "When you guys freed the spirits, she had a total meltdown—an all-out, tree-tossing-rock-smashing hissy fit. I'm surprised you didn't hear her. Her power would be kind of cool if she weren't so damn freaky. She took off down the paths to find you guys, so I turned back into my misty self and sunk into the ground."

"How come you can be in the tunnels but Mary can't?" I ask. "Does it hurt?"

"It feels...wrong being underneath here, but it doesn't hurt," Roman says. "But I only have a little blood and hair buried underneath the tree. Mary has her entire body, so it must be torture to go underground."

We fill Roman in on the network of tunnels before Mary's banshee cries fill the air.

"She's back," Roman says. The new holes in the dirt ceiling make it easier to hear what's going on above ground.

"Now what?" Jake tenses up and clenches his fists, like he's ready to leap into the ring with Mary and duke it out.

Roman looks between Jake and me with a grin on his face. "How about we really make Mary mad?"

"Isn't she already mad?" I arch an eyebrow and wait for the rest of his plan.

"We're going to set some more souls free." Jake grins back at his little brother.

"Not just some," Roman adds. "We're going to release them all."

"How?" I ask as soil starts lightly raining on our heads.

"We'll use this tunnel and pull them down from the ceiling, just like you did with the keys," Roman says.

"Are you sure it's sturdy enough?" I ask. A large clump of clay falls from above and lands near my feet.

Suddenly, everything is quiet, so quiet I can hear the dirt falling around us.

Jake reaches for me and yells, "Run!"

That's the last thing I hear before everything goes black.

Chapter 21
CAN'T BREATHE

MY PARENTS TOOK ROMAN AND ME SNOWMOBILING IN THE mountains last winter. Before they'd let us on the sled, we had to take an avalanche preparedness course.

"If you get caught in an avalanche, swim through the snow in the area you want to go," the instructor had said calmly, like swimming through tons of snow was a totally normal thing to do.

His voice rings in my head as a wave of earth smacks into my back, sending me toppling forward into the already knee-high dirt. The sides of the dirt tunnel collapse. I try swimming through the sea of dirt and snarled roots, but it doesn't help. Dirt rushes over my head and plugs my ears. I scramble to get my feet on the ground, so I have something to push off of. I can feel the cavern trembling as more dirt shakes free.

It's so heavy—too heavy. I can't move. Dirt crowds my nostrils, and I open my mouth to scream. It pours into my mouth, and suddenly I can't breathe. My lungs start to smolder.

I can't breathe.

I can't breathe.

I can't br—

Ice cold hands grab me under my armpits and haul me forward. My head breaks free, and I spit out the dirt in my mouth before gasping for air.

Roman tugs my arms until my legs are free. I stumble into the dark, empty tunnel. A light flashes in my face. It's Jake.

"Are you okay?" He asks. His face is covered in streaks of mud, but he's okay.

I nod and spit again. "I'm okay, I think."

Roman grabs my arm and helps me up. "Let's get out of here before any more tunnels cave in."

I stand up, tears pricking the backs of my eyes, but I won't cry. Not now. Not when we're still in danger.

We run through the tunnels until we burst through a small, wooden door. We find ourselves in the basement of the library on Main Street.

We torpedo ourselves up the stairs and walk right into Ms. Young.

Her eyes widen as big as the dancing bulldogs on her sweater vest.

"I have a feeling I don't want to know what you three are up to," she says.

I shake my head, making dirt rain down on my shoulders. "Probably not."

She clasps my chin in her warm, wrinkled hand. "Are you alright?"

I nod.

"Then get out of here. You're filthy," she says gently. "And I mean go home, Elsie. You look like you could use a rest."

"That's the understatement of the year," I mutter.

We spill out onto the street and into the sunshine.

"My parents aren't home," Jake says. "Let's go there."

—

When we get there, I call first dibs on the shower. Jake lends me some clothes while I throw mine in the wash. When we're cleaned up, we all go downstairs to the rec room, claim a couch and fall asleep.

I wake up to Roman's ice-pick fingers tapping my shoulder.

"Hey, where'd Jake go?" He asks.

I rub the goobers out of my eyes and look around. "I don't know. Where were you?"

"I was upstairs in my room. Jake was here when I left, but he's gone now. I even checked the treehouse, and he's not there." Roman paces in front of me.

"Relax," I say. "I'm sure he's around here somewhere. I'll check the backyard again."

I stretch and roll off the couch. I grab my clothes out of the drier and pull them on. I wander into the backyard, and I find a sheet of white paper flickering from the trap door of the tree house. Jake left us a note. Of course Roman missed it—he would've floated up to the window rather than taking the shaky rope ladder that leads to the trap door.

I climb the ladder and grab the thick piece of paper, already imagining the lame reason Jake left without saying something. Except it's not paper. I climb down and examine it. It's a piece of Jake's white T-shirt with a huge, red mark on it.

"Did you find him?" Roman asks, his chin hovering over my shoulder, his breath cool on my cheek.

I lift the scrap of bloody fabric. "When Mary caught me, she said she was going to bleed me dry. He wouldn't have gone to…did Mary take…no…she's too weak…right? Right?"

Roman grabs my shoulder and spins me around. "We need to go. Right now."

Waves of panic crash into the walls of my chest, and all of a sudden, I feel like I'm drowning, again. We can't handle this on our own; it's too much.

"We need help, Roman. Mary might k-kill him. We can't stop her on our own." Big, fat tears run down my cheeks, and I can't blink fast enough to stop them.

"Hey, it's going to be okay." Roman drops down and wipes my face with the backs of his fingertips.

"What if we're too late?" I whisper.

"We won't be," Roman says. "Now you're going to hop on your bike, and we're going to go find him, kay?"

I nod and grab my bike off the ground. I wheel it out of the yard and onto the sidewalk. I push off the pavement and pedal as hard as I possibly can. My legs are on fire before I reach the end of the block. I keep my eyes open, but I pray the entire way to the graveyard that this is all a mistake.

If Mary thinks that she can hurt Jake, just so she can stick around, she has another thing coming. She's already gotten her chance to live—she doesn't get to use someone else's blood or energy just because she doesn't want to cross over. That's not how life works. Or death works, or whatever it is. When your time's up, it's up.

Maybe Roman can be the exception?

By the time we reach the cemetery, I'm not scared anymore, I'm just mad. I scramble over the fence and start down the path.

"Let's go kick some ghost butt."

Chapter 22
MARY'S COMING

WE SPLIT UP, EVEN THOUGH IT'S AGAINST EVERY RULE drilled into my brain from hours of horror movies. I stick to the path while Roman disappears into the trees. He needs to either lure Mary away from the Bone Tree or patrol the area around it to make sure she stays away. I need to find Jake.

The remaining sun makes every leaf, twig and branch turn to gold, and for a split second, I forget that I'm about to face a terrifying banshee.

A screech resembling a zillion nails on a chalkboard fills the air. My stomach turns to lead. I walk as lightly as I can, careful not to trip and face-plant on the way. When the Bone Tree comes into view, I want to turn around and run. I don't, obviously, but every brain cell screams for me to get the heck out of here.

Jake is tied to the Bone Tree like a pirate around a ship's mast. There's a cut on his cheek, and his torn collar is bloody, but he's in one piece. I let out a huge breath. I'm not too late.

Just to be safe, I creep over a huge, angel-shaped head-stone. I crouch behind it and peek through a bush made of jagged thorns that threaten my eyeballs each time I breathe.

"Let me go," Jake hollers at his invisible kidnapper. "Or I'll burn the tree down and your bones with it!"

Great, now is not the time to tick Mary off.

"Jake," I stage whisper as loud as I can.

Jake lets out an angry cry and yanks at the ancient, thick rope wrapped around his waist.

"Jake, shut up, will ya!" I scamper out of my hiding spot and crawl behind the tree. Before Jake can make another peep, I reach around and clamp my hand over his mouth. He shuts up for five seconds, but only so he can bite me. "Ouch!"

I let go of his mouth and stick my head around the trunk. "Els?" Jake gasps. "What are you doing here?"

"Saving your butt. Do you have a knife or anything?" I ask.

Jake rolls his eyes at me. "When is life ever that easy?"

"Good point." I look around the ground for a sharp rock, but there's nothing but flat, smooth stones. An ear-piercing whistle comes from somewhere up above. "Crap."

"What's wrong?" Jake strains against the ropes. "Other than the obvious."

"That was my signal to get you out of here." I purse my lips and whistle a two-note melody before I bend down and gnaw on the rope so hard strands of the scratchy fibers get caught in my teeth. I feel like I'm the spy on one of those movies you can only see with your parents. Only I'm not feeling as brave as they seem. "Can you wiggle your hands?"

Jake twists his hands, and his skin poking out from under the rope quickly turns pink then red. "Is it helping?"

"Not really." I want to slide down the tree and cry. I want to give up, but I can't. "Just stay here, and I'll look for something to cut the ropes."

"It's not like I have a choice," Jake says. His eyes let me know that the sarcastic, tough guy thing is just an act. He's totally freaking out.

"I'll be right back. I promise." I leave him, only going a few steps away, and search for a piece of a demolished gravestone. I find a jagged piece of rock and hold it up triumphantly. I run back to Jake and saw through the first layer of rope.

"You're my hero," Jake says and flashes me his absolute best smile.

My grip slips, and the pointy end tears a hole in his T-shirt. "Whoops."

Now is definitely not the time to be distracted. I focus on sawing through the rest of the rope, and I somehow get Jake free without gutting him in the process.

Another coyote-like howl tears through the air.

Roman plummets to the ground and lands in an Iron Man squat at the last minute. "Mary's coming."

We take off, running as fast as we can down a path none of us have taken before. Roman swirls around us, constantly swooping up and down, making sure the coast is clear.

We follow Roman down the trail. Jake's attention swivels between the path behind us and the sky above us.

———

A worn down, old house marks the end of the trail. Its windows are boarded up, there are holes in the porch and there's not a light in sight.

"Should we backtrack down the path?" I ask.

"Mary's going down a different path." Roman joins us on the ground and points at the house. "But she'll catch up fast, so we better get out of here."

The trees just a couple hundred feet away start to shake.

"We don't have time to run." Jake grabs my hand and pulls me up the porch stairs.

We burst through the front door and look for a place to hide among the garbage and dirt.

"This must be the Simon family's house while they were caretakers." I nudge a broken wooden chair with the tip of my sneaker. More old, stained furniture covers the ground along with an inch of dust. Dirty dishes sit in an old-school sink—the kind you need a bucket to fill—making the whole place smell like mold and grease. A bare mattress is pushed into the corner of the room, there isn't a blanket or pillow in sight.

"Charming," Roman says. "And pretty much impossible to hide in."

"Guys," Jake hisses from the back of the living room. "There's got to be a basement. She can't go underground, remember?"

I catch a glimpse of a white blur soaring up onto the porch. Roman and Jake scatter in search of a safe place while I look for the basement door that I know must be hidden in the floorboards—somewhere around here. I run my hands along the wall, but I can't feel anything. Only a solitary sunbeam shines through the window. It helps about as much as the tiny tea lights Mom keeps around the bathtub.

"Mary is upstairs," Roman whispers. "I can feel her."

"We need to hide." Jake waves me over to a stack of wooden crates.

"Roman, can you see if there's a tunnel?" I whisper.

Roman nods and transforms into his misty self. He dissolves into the walls.

I tiptoe over to Jake, and we crouch behind the stack of crates. We press our back against the wall. My heart beats so hard I wonder if Jake can feel it vibrating through the wood. Somewhere upstairs a door swings open and slams against the wall. I squeak and grab onto Jake's arm. He holds a finger in front of his mouth and points upward.

"You may have taken the boy away, but I'll find another," Mary says in a creepy sing-song voice. "The town is full of snot-nosed, little brats with more than enough blood to spill. I just need one or two to get infatuated with the Bone Tree, just like you, my dearies."

"I found a tunnel," Roman whispers as he steps out of the wall and walks along it, staring at the floor the entire time. "There is a hidden latch that releases the door along the ground somewhere around here."

Jake and I join him in the search. I find it a minute later and pull it. The door creaks open loudly, too loudly. We all freeze.

"I heard that!" Mary screeches.

"Get in the tunnel," I whisper and wave Roman and Jake into the impossibly black hole. I go in last and shut the door behind us and let the darkness swallow us whole. Jake lights up his phone as a flashlight, hands it to me and we run into the dark tunnel without looking back.

I follow Roman, and Jake follows me. We twist and turn, going deeper and deeper into the underground labyrinth.

We slow down to a jog when I'm sure we're far enough away.

"There should be another door around here somewhere." I gasp for air.

"Silly, child…" Mary's whisper bounces off the tunnel walls, filling my head with her voice. "You cannot run from me. I'll have your blood one way or another."

"This way!" Roman shouts. He grabs my hand and yanks me left.

Jake yelps from behind me.

I grab him, and we run toward a faintly lit door at the end of the tunnel.

Jake reaches the door first.

I stop him from opening it. "What if this drops us off the falls or something?"

"Then hold your breath before you hit the water." Jake grabs the tiny doorknob and twists it. The door swings open soundlessly, and it takes me a second before my eyes adjust.

"I know where we are." I squint and double-check.

"Are we safe here?" Roman steps in and looks around the storage room full of tiny chairs and props.

"There's nowhere safer for us to be." I smile at the guys. "We're in a church."

Jake closes the tunnel door and opens the storage room door. We spill into the empty church basement.

"We messed up." I cover my face with my hands. "Now instead of burying tokens, she's going to kill kids."

"We'll figure something out before that happens." Roman pulls my hands down. "I promise."

"Hey Els, does my phone have any battery left?" Jake asks.

"Yeah, why?" I whirl around and look at Jake. There's a pale, crooked branch protruding from his shoulder.

"Ya might wanna call someone," he says.

"Oh my gosh, what happened?" I run over and put my hands on either side of the branch. His shirt is sticky with blood.

"Mary chucked it at me when I was running," Jake grunts. He reaches for the branch, but I gently push his hand down. "I think she was going for you, but I got in her way."

"So much for her not being able to use the tunnels." Roman hovers around Jake. "Els, you need to call 911. Now."

"Relax, Roman. I'm totally fine," Jake says right before his eyes roll back into his head, and he collapses into a heap.

Chapter 23

WE NEED TO TALK

I GRAB JAKE AND PULL HIM INTO A SITTING POSITION. His face is pale and gleaming with sweat.

I call 911 and tell them where we are. I ignore the operator when she tells me to stay on the phone, and I hang up.

"I'm going to watch for the ambulance," Roman says. He looks like he's about to cry.

I lightly smack Jake's cheeks.

"Jake. Hey Jake, wake up," I say frantically.

Jakes eyes flutter open. "You need to get out of here."

"What?" I ask, pulling Jake's back into my chest. "No way."

He leans his head back onto my shoulder and looks at me. "Yes, way. You're the worst liar I've ever met. It'll be hard enough trying to come up with a story about what happened on my own, let alone with you here."

Roman appears in front of us. "I can hear the sirens already, so just hang on, Jake."

"Get Elsie out of here," Jake wheezes. "If her parents find out she was with me, you guys won't be able to stop Mary."

"Good point," Roman says. "Come on, Els, we can sneak out the back door."

"Okay." I give in and ease Jake off of me and lean him against the basement wall. I hear the paramedics stomping upstairs. "He's down here!"

I look at Jake one more time before following Roman out the secret back door that leads us outside—the last place we should probably be.

We walk to my house in silence. My stomach is in knots because I know Roman has a terrible idea of how we're going to stop Mary, and I don't want to hear it.

———

When we get to my house, I walk in the front door and try to act like everything is fine. Luckily my sweatshirt is black; otherwise, my parents would see smears of blood.

"Hey, kiddo," Mom says. "You're just in time for dinner."

"Great," I say weakly. "I'm starving."

"How was Ashleigh's?" Dad asks. He sets a big roast down on the table.

Is that where I said I was?

"It was good," I lie.

"Glad to hear it," Dad says. "Want some potatoes?"

"I'm going to go check on Jake." Roman drifts toward the door. "I'll get him to email you from the hospital."

I nod slightly and pick at my food. If Jake's not okay, I don't know what I'm going to do. Losing one Pierce brother was hard enough.

—

The phone rings an hour after we finish dinner. Mom answers, and judging by her escalating voice, it's Mrs. Pierce telling her Jake's in the hospital.

I try to focus on the lame TV show, Dad and I are watching, until my mom finally comes into the living room.

"Els, hon, before I tell you what happened, I just want you to know that Jake is going to be fine." Mom sits next to me on the couch and pauses the show.

I force my eyes to widen in pretend shock. "What are you talking about?"

"There was an accident," she says. "Jake and some friends were fooling around in an old church basement, and he slipped and fell into a stack of broken pews."

The story is an obvious lie. "Oh no, is he alright?"

"He got a chunk of wood right through his shoulder, but he's going to be okay."

"Can I go see him?" I jump off the couch. I'm not faking this time. I really do want to see with my own eyes if Jake's okay.

Mom shakes her head. "They've given him some pretty

strong pain medication, so he's going to spend the night at the hospital. Mrs. Pierce said you can go visit him in the morning."

I groan. "I have to wait that long?"

Mom laughs softly. "Sorry, kid. He's had to get quite a few stitches, so he's probably passed out. I'll take you over once we get word that he's home."

"It'll be good for you to go hang out there again," Dad says. "I know you've been planning on spending some time with Roman's parents, so this will be a good excuse. Try to steal me a pan of Mrs. Pierce's lasagna while you're over there, will ya?"

"I'll give it a shot," I grumble. I hate that I have to wait before I can see Jake—weird. I never thought I'd be bummed over Jake Pierce.

—

When I head to my room, I grab my laptop and check my email. There's a message from Jake.

"Els, spending the night here. Only needed ten stitches. Girls still like scars, right? lol. Roman is staying with me. Come over tomorrow. Stay put. Night."

I reread the message a few times before I close my computer and climb into bed. Part of me wishes Roman were here in case Mary gets any funny ideas, but the other part of me is happy he's with Jake. He'll need all the help he can get if Mary tries to finish the job.

—

Mom takes me to the Pierce's first thing the next morning. I jump out of the car before it's fully stopped and fly up the walkway. I bang on the door, probably a little harder than I need to, and wait.

Mrs. Pierce answers the door. Her face is pale, and her eyes are red, but she gives me a smile and a hug anyway.

"It's good to see you, Elsie," she says. "One of these times it's going to have to be under better circumstances."

"It's good to see you too," I say. "Is Jake awake?"

She nods. "He's set up in the rec room downstairs. Can you let me know if he needs anything? The doctor doesn't want him moving around too much."

"Will do," I say.

I cut through the kitchen and jog down the stairs and into the rec room. Jake is sprawled out on the sectional, surrounded by stacks of pillows and blankets. He's got a T-shirt on but thick, white bandages poke out of his collar and climb up his neck.

"Hey," he says quietly. "I didn't know if you were going to come over or not."

I plop down beside him. "I wanted to come over earlier, but Mom made me wait until your mom called." I look around the room. "Where's Roman?"

Jake shrugs and instantly winces. "Probably with Dad. He's in my room trying to prop up my bed to make it more comfortable for me to sleep on. Last I saw, Dad was carrying in a drill."

"Oh jeez," I say. "Roman is probably the least helpful person to assist with a renovation."

Jake laughs and then winces again. "Yeah, he's just kinda floating around my room. Dad's been...I don't know...different since last night. It's like seeing me in the hospital made him wake up a bit. He seems more like the dad I had when Roman was alive."

I reach over and squeeze Jake's arm.

"Does that make me a bad person?" Jake asks. "To be happy that my dad was so freaked out about my accident that he's back to almost normal?"

"No way," I say. "You need him. I'm happy he sees that."

Jake sighs and sinks back into the couch. "So what are we going to do about Mary?"

Roman appears out of nowhere and settles down next to Jake. "Yeah, about that. We need to talk."

Chapter 24

CINNAMON AND FABRIC SOFTENER

THE SINKING FEELING IN MY GUT TELLS ME THAT I'M NOT going to like what Roman has to say. Not one bit.

"Guys," he starts. "I think we all know what I need to do."

I hold up my hands. "No. Don't say it."

"We can't keep trying to free the ghosts one at a time… it's not working," Roman says.

"Then we'll come up with a better way," I say. "There are all those Bobcat tractors all over the graveyard. We can steal one of those and dig up like a hundred tokens at once."

"Who's going to drive it?" He asks. "You?"

"I will," Jake says. "I just need a few days."

"Even if that did work, there's no way we could do that without Mary showing up. Look what she did to you, Jake. We can't go back to the Bone Tree just to dig up tokens. It's too risky," Roman says. "All it takes is one adult spotting us digging around the cemetery, and you'll be grounded for life."

"We'll find a way," I say.

"Okay, say we find a way to clear out all the tokens without Mary catching or hurting one of us again," he says. "Then what? Are you going to spend the rest of your life making sure no one buries anything under the Bone Tree?"

I nod so hard my teeth clink together. "Jake and I will do it. We'll go every Wednesday or something."

"Forever?" Roman reaches over and squeezes my hand. "You can't spend the rest of your life hovering around some old tree."

"Yes I can, especially if it means keeping you here," I say.

Roman smiles a little. "Weren't you the one who said Samuel was wasting his life in the graveyard? That he could've moved on instead of spending his life in the dark and the dirt?"

"That's different, and you know it," I shoot back. "You're not even giving us an option," I say.

Roman just shrugs.

"Then what's your brilliant idea? We're going to dig old Mary up? Then all the ghosts will cross over, and we won't have to worry about the tree ever again?" I ask. I'm so sad and mad that the combination is making my head swim and my stomach ache, all at once.

"That's kinda exactly what I was thinking," Roman says.

My heart hurts so bad that it feels like it's actually cracking and snapping off into chunks.

"You know what that means when you cross over too, right? That you'll leave me, Jake, and your parents all over again, you know that, right?" I'm crying now, but I don't care. Roman deserves to see how wrecked I'll be if he leaves me again.

"You don't have to leave, Roman. You know we'd do anything for you," Jake says. "Even if it does mean going back to the graveyard every day."

"Okay, so that's fine for now. But what about five years from now? Are you giving up your dream of going to art school, Els? Because last time I checked there weren't any great art proGrams in Fredric Falls." Roman stands up and paces in front of the couch. "What about you, Jake? You always said you were moving to Costa Rica for a year after graduating high school. Who's going to dig up the tokens when you're surfing in some tiny village?"

"That's not going to happen for a really long time," Jake says. "We'll figure something out."

"Don't you get it?" Roman snaps. "You guys are going to move on with your lives. I don't get to get my driver's license. I don't get to travel or go to college. You guys are going to keep growing up, and I'm going to stay stuck like this…forever."

Neither Jake nor I say a word.

Roman sits back down. "I know I made you bring me back, Els. We've all tried so hard to keep me around, but things are different now. People can get hurt—Jake has already been hurt. You've been hurt. I won't risk either of you guys getting hurt again, just so I can drag out being twelve a little longer. This is the only way."

"No, it's not," I say. "We can just leave the tree and Mary alone. We'll never go back, and everything will be fine."

"So you're okay with all those souls dying over and over again, just so I can stick around?" He asks.

I fight the urge to chuck a pillow at his head. "Yes."

Roman shakes his head. "You're a terrible liar."

I bury my face in my hands. "There has to be a better way."

Roman hugs me and rests his cheek on my head. "This is the best way, Els. I get to save all those spirits and cross over as a total hero. Captain America will have nothing on me."

I cry harder, and Roman stops talking. I sit in between Jake and Roman, crying like a baby until the hallway creaks with footsteps.

"Jake, buddy, you okay in there?" Mr. Pierce steps into the rec room. "Elsie, I didn't know you were here. I was just wondering who Jake was talking to."

I dry my eyes as fast as I can. Mr. Pierce pretends he doesn't see my tears.

"Hiya, Mr. P," I say as brightly as I can.

Mr. Pierce wipes grease-smudged hands on his jeans. "I was just coming out here to see if Jake wanted me to order pizza for lunch and watch a movie. You're more than welcome to join us."

"That sounds great," I say.

Roman stares at his Dad. "He seems so…happy today."

A thud comes from upstairs.

"Oh no," Mr. Pierce sighs. "I better go check on your mother."

I give Jake a questioning look.

"Mom's probably going through Roman's closet again," he says. "She does that at least once a week."

"Can I go see her?" I ask.

Mr. Pierce thinks for a minute before nodding. "Sure. Hawaiian pizza okay?"

I nod. "That's the best."

I grab Roman and pull him up the stairs.

—

Mrs. Pierce is, indeed, in Roman's closet. She's sitting inside with a box labeled "summer clothes" opened in her lap.

I knock on the doorframe. "Can I come in?"

Mrs. Pierce looks up, startled and a little embarrassed. "Of course, honey. I was just going through some of Roman's old things."

Roman and I sit on the edge of his bed. I pull one of his pillows into my lap and bury my face in it, but it doesn't smell like Roman anymore. Even though he's right next to me, I miss the old him so much it makes my cried-out eyes burn.

"It doesn't smell like him anymore," she says from the closet floor. "I'm not sure when it stopped. I came in here one day, and the smell of him was just gone. I can't find it anywhere. Not a single T-shirt or sweatshirt, even his socks just smell like normal cotton. I...I know that makes me sound like I'm crazy—smelling his socks and all—but I just miss him so much."

"I miss him too," I murmur.

Roman floats off the bed and settles on the floor next to his mom.

"When Roman got sick, I started thinking about all the last times I'd have with him. Like the last time I'd get to kiss his forehead before he went to bed or stay up late watching movies. I knew we'd have a last laugh, and I'd tell him how much I loved him one more time. But I never thought about the last time I'd smell his hair when he hugged me."

A fat tear rolls down my cheek.

Mrs. Pierce shoves her hands in the box of clothes. "I thought that maybe I'd be able to catch a bit of his scent, just one last time, but these just smell like dust."

I crawl off the bed and sit across from Mrs. Pierce. I take her hand and give her my best smile. "We'll just have to come up with other ways to remember him."

"I think I might be able to help," Roman says. "Just give me a second."

Roman squeezes his eyes as if he's concentrating on the world's hardest math problem.

"He was a good boy, wasn't he?" she whispers.

I squeeze her hand. "He was the best."

She reaches up and tugs down Roman's favorite red sweatshirt off a hanger—the zip-up one he wears in his semi-after life. "Sometimes, I think if I hug this hard enough, a little piece of him will come back to me."

Roman grins at me, and suddenly the air explodes with tinges of cinnamon and fabric softener.

Mrs. Pierce gasps and dissolves into tears—only these tears don't sound sad, they sound happy.

"I've got this," Roman says. He leans against his mom and wraps his arms around her shoulders.

I sit with them for a few minutes as she laugh-cries into Roman's sweatshirt, completely unaware that Roman is with her. I stand up from the floor and give Roman some time alone with his mom.

I head back downstairs and into the rec room with my heart so full it feels like my ribs will burst.

Mr. Pierce is sitting next to Jake, gently rearranging the pillow under Jake's arm before ruffling his son's hair like he's a little boy again. They both smile and look back at the TV—some terrible made-for-TV action movie.

I clear my throat and hop over the back of the sectional.

"Pizza should be here soon," Jake says. "How's mom?"

"She's good," I say, giving them both a smile.

We watch the movie for ten or so minutes before the doorbell rings. Before Mr. Pierce can get off the couch, Mrs. Pierce comes down the stairs with the pizza. Roman drifts behind her with a grin a mile wide covering his face.

"Room for one more?" Mrs. Pierce asks, settling down beside me.

"There always is," I say.

Everyone grabs a slice, and for the first time in a long time, I think we all might be okay.

Chapter 25

DOUBLE CRAP

WHEN THE MOVIE IS OVER, MR. AND MRS. PIERCE EXCUSE themselves to go upstairs for a nap. Jake takes another dose of his pain meds before Roman gets that look on his face again.

"Not again," I groan. "Can't we just enjoy one nice evening."

"Not when there's a chance of more souls being enslaved," Roman says. He even has the guts to wink at me. "I know Jake is out of commission, but we need to make a game plan in case Mary pulls something. I'm not saying that anything needs to happen right this second, but I need you two to agree that if we need to pull the trigger and take out Mary, that you'll do it."

I look at Jake. There's no point in arguing with Roman anymore. If we don't agree to help him, Roman is going to do something careless.

Jake must've read my mind, because he sighs and says, "Okay. Let's come up with Operation Kill Switch."

I groan, "I'm never watching another action movie with either of you again."

As Jake and Roman go over details of the plan, I steal Jake's phone and check my Snapchat streak. And bam! Just like that, my good mood is ruined.

Ashleigh's most recent Snap reads, "Carlee, Levi and I are going ghost hunting in the cemetery tonight!"

Crap. Crap. Crap.

"Do you guys mind if I take off? I have to swing by Ashleigh's house and drop off her birthday present. She's still pretty mad I didn't go to her birthday party, so I don't want to make her wait for her present too," I say.

"Sure," Roman says. "I'll come by your house later."

"Or just come back here when you're done," Jake says. "I think Mom's making fajitas."

I paste a smile on my face. "Great, sounds good."

I head toward the door that leads into the backyard.

Double crap.

"Let me guess," Jake says. "You need to borrow my bike?"

"Can I?" I ask.

He nods.

"Thanks!" I open the sliding door and close it behind me. I grab Jake's bike and wheel it out the backyard before I climb on and pedal out of the yard. I cut through back alleys and a park until I'm in front of Ashleigh's house. I run to the side of the house and knock on her bedroom window.

She slides it open and steps back for me to climb through it.

"Hey," I say totally out of breath.

"Elsie, what are you doing here?" She asks, looking genuinely surprised. "And dude…you know I've got a front door, right?"

"This couldn't wait for parents. I saw that you were going to the graveyard tonight," I pant. "That's a bad idea. You can't go there—it's too dangerous."

Ashleigh rolls her eyes. "Since when do you care about what we do?"

I blink. "What's that supposed to mean?"

She sighs and grabs my shoulders. "I know losing Roman was hard on you. It was really hard on all of us, but since he died, you've just dropped off the face of the earth. The twins and I haven't seen you at all. And when you didn't come to my birthday… well, that really sucked."

"I'm sorry," I say lamely.

"Honestly, it felt like we lost both you and Roman," she says, letting go of my shoulders.

"I really am sorry," I say. "I know I haven't been around, but I'll try harder. I promise."

"Good." Ashleigh grins. "You can start by coming to the graveyard tomorrow night. Carlee and Levi's mom was talking about the old legend about the ghost that supposedly haunts the graveyard, so we're going to check it out."

"I thought you were going tonight," I blurt out.

"We were, but Levi has some dumb math test he has to study for. He just texted me two minutes ago, bailing to hit the books," she says.

"Listen to me," I say. "You guys can't go to the graveyard. I can't explain, but there's some bad stuff going on there."

Ashleigh rolls her eyes again. "Don't tell me you actually believe those stories."

"They're not just stories," I insist. "Just promise me you won't go."

Ashleigh purses her lips and thinks for a minute. "No, I think we're going to check it out."

My mouth drops open. "You can't!"

"Just because you finally have time for me doesn't mean you get to boss me around too," she says. "You better go. My mom will get mad if she knows my uh, friends are still sneaking in through my window. Carlee kicked a lamp over last time so…"

"Please don't go," I say one more time.

"If you're really that freaked out about our safety then come with us." Ashleigh opens the window and holds her curtains to the side.

I climb out the window, my entire body completely numb. They're going to the Bone Tree—to Mary—whether I want them to or not. If Mary's desperate enough, she may bleed all three of them out just for some extra power—power that Jake, Roman and I took away from her.

I grab Jake's bike off of Ashleigh's front lawn and climb on it. I know what I have to do.

I, Elsie Edwards, am going to take care of Mary once and for all.

Chapter 26

OVER AND OUT

I SWING BY THE HOUSE, QUICKLY LIE TO MY PARENTS about where I'm going and stuff my backpack full of a few essentials. I take my own bike in case Jake somehow comes looking for his, and I head down a now all-too-familiar route.

When I come to the graveyard, I take the same path I always do. As I walk down it, I try to imagine that I'm Harry Potter, and I have the resurrection stone. I call Roman to me and imagine he's here, encouraging me and telling me everything is going to be okay. But when the path ends, and the tree comes into view, I remember that I'm alone, and everything is definitely not going to be okay.

The Bone Tree stands alone, cloaked in swirling fog, but I know Mary is close by. I stand under the tree, my back pressed against the cool trunk, and I close my eyes.

"Mary Simon!" I shout. "I have a deal to make with you!"

"What's this?" Mary hisses in my ear. She floats into view and hovers right in front of my face. "The little soul snatcher has a deal for me?"

"I know you want my blood," I say. I force myself to stare into her black, oozing eyes. "And I'll give it to you, but only if you agree to something."

Mary arches her head backward and cackles. It sounds like claws scraping across a chalkboard. "What would you like from me?"

"I want you to let me dig up all the tokens," I say. "And you have to promise to never use another spirit's energy again. If you let me take the tokens, I'll give you some of my blood. I'll just have to trust that you won't use any more tokens."

"How do I know that your blood will work for me the same way it worked for your little friend?" she asks.

Her breath is hot and smells like rotten eggs and fire. "I'm related to you. Your husband is my great-great-great-great uncle or something. If my blood worked on Roman, someone I'm not even related to, it will definitely work for you."

Mary taps a talon on her chin. The tip pierces her molted skin, and a tiny river of black ooze seeps out. "So I let you take the tokens, and you'll give me some of your blood?"

My brain screams at me to run and bile slithers up my throat, but I nod and pull out Roman's Swiss Army knife. "Yes."

"But what's to stop me from just taking your blood any-way?" Mary whispers softly.

I reach into my pocket and pull open a handful of salt packets. "If you try that, I'll get away and never come back. I'll send so many people here to dig up the tokens that you won't be able to stop us all."

Mary stares at me, her eyes gleaming in the moonlight. She purses her lips and blows. Air gusts out of her lungs so hard that the salt packets fly out of my hand, whip into the air and scatter throughout the tombstones.

"Now let me see your pretty little arm," she purrs.

Oh, crap.

"I'll do it," I snap. I'll have to come back and get the tokens another way. Right now, all I need to do is get out of here. I push my sweatshirt sleeve up and flick open the tiny knife. "Do you want the blood anywhere special?"

"Oh no, child," she says. She flies toward me and grabs both my arms in an iron grip. "You must let me do the honors."

The knife falls to the ground as Mary jerks me forward. Her pointed nails dig into my arms and blood wells up around them. She lets one arm go and drags a claw down my forearm.

I hiss from the pain and try to pull my arm away. Her grip tightens.

Blood pours out of the cut, dripping onto the exposed roots of the Bone Tree.

"There," I grunt. "That's good enough."

Mary tsks, opening another cut on my other arm. "I think we better take it all, just to be safe."

"W-what?" I stammer. "But that'll kill me."

Mary gives me a gruesome smile. Her teeth are gray and rotten, those that are left that is. "That is the plan, foolish girl."

My head swims, and I finally realize how stupid I am. Of course she'll want all of my blood—why did I think that there was any good left in her?

"Please don't," I whisper. "My parents…Jake…I don't know what they'll do without me."

"You should've thought about that before you came to the cemetery to bargain." Mary yanks me down one of the trails. "Now come along before you bleed out. I have a few special places I want you to mark."

Mary drags me down narrow, twisting paths. She stops every once in a while, smearing my arms across broken tombstones and sagging tree limbs.

Each step gets a little harder. Every minute that passes gets a little dimmer. The bleeding on my right arm starts to slow, so she opens another cut along my bicep.

Tears fall down my cheeks, mixing with the warm blood on my arms. We're heading back to the Bone Tree now. My feet drag through piles of dry leaves. My arms feel like they're on fire. The tree comes into view, and Mary lets go of me.

She shoves me forward, and I tumble to the ground.

"There," she says, pointing to the white, snarled roots. "You can finish there."

By finish, she means die. I struggle into a sitting position and try to stop the bleeding. It leaks through my fingers anyway.

My eyelids feel like they have tiny weights strapped to

them. I want to close my eyes and rest for a minute, but I know that's not a good idea. I force myself to think of Mom and Dad, Roman and Jake, Ashleigh and the twins. I bite the inside of my cheek to keep myself awake and squeeze the cuts tighter so the bleeding will stop.

Mary looks at me struggling and laughs. Her laugh grows louder and louder until she's howling. And then screaming.

"What have you done?" she shrieks.

Roman appears from behind the Bone Tree, his arms full of yellowish white branches. Only they're not branches—they're bones.

"She didn't do anything except try to let you stick around a little longer," Roman says.

"No!" Mary cries. "What are you doing!"

"What I should've done a long time ago," Roman says. "It's not right for us to stay here when staying means others have to suffer."

Roman drops the bones, and Jake comes up behind him with a plastic bottle of water. He dumps it on the bones, and they begin to sizzle and steam. He doesn't stop—even when the bones fizzle and deteriorate in front of our eyes.

Jake rushes over to me. "I took some holy water from the hospital chapel before I left. I think it's doing the trick."

Mary drops to the ground and thrashes in the dried, crackling leaves.

"What's happening to her?" I ask.

"She's crossing over." Roman kneels next to me and squeezes my hand.

Mary howls and rolls on the ground like an alligator in a death spin. Steam rises off her body and chunks of flesh start to fly off her arms and legs. The more she spins and rolls, the more skin peels off until she's nothing but a skeleton. And then dust. And then nothing at all.

The pain in my arms takes over, and I let out a groan.

Jake rips open his backpack and pulls out a handful of bandages. "What were you thinking, Elsie? Remember the original plan? You were supposed to distract Mary while Roman and I found her bones. That's it. You weren't supposed to offer your blood. And you definitely weren't supposed to start the plan while I still had a hole in my shoulder."

He's right. I shouldn't have launched Operation Kill Switch without them.

"Ashleigh and the twins were going to come to the Bone Tree. I had to do something. I thought Mary would agree to my deal," I say. "Since my blood replaces the need for tokens, I thought she'd let me dig them up for a little bit of it…but she wanted it all."

Roman sucks in a breath. "You could've died, Els."

I look up at him. "I know. I'm sorry, I couldn't stop thinking about losing you, and it made me a little desperate."

"What the heck?" Roman looks at the bandages on my arms only there's no blood on any of them. Not even a speck.

I flex my arms, and there's not a single hint of pain. *So strange.*

"Jake, how do you feel?" I ask.

"Good. Why?" Jake pauses and then looks at this shoulder. "The hole...it's gone."

"It's like Mary's crossing over took away her damage," I say. *Which means it will probably take the magic too.* The realization makes my throat close up.

"There is another way." A young woman steps out of the lingering fog. She's tanned with freckles across her nose. Her cheeks are rosy, and her hair hangs down in messy, beautiful brown curls. "The magic of the Bone Tree is fading quickly. Unless you recreate the witch's blessing, Roman will cross over. I can show you how if you'd like?"

I recognize the woman from pictures in that old dusty book—Mary. The real Mary. Before the Bone Tree and the magic. Here, in this moment, she isn't evil, with sagging skin, and talons for nails. She's beautiful.

"Yes!" I shout. "Please show us how to do it."

"Can I have a minute?" Roman asks the woman.

"Of course," Mary says.

Roman, Jake and I walk around to the other side of the Bone Tree.

"Guys," Roman says. "I can't stay."

Jake looks down at his shoes and stuffs his hands in his pockets. His shoulder is covered in thick, white bandages that are no longer needed. "Why? She said you could."

"Then what?" Roman kicks a rock. "I can watch you guys grow up and graduate, become grown-ups. But nothing's going to change for me. I'll be stuck like this forever."

My heart hurts so much it's impossible to talk. I grab Roman's hand, drop to my knees in front of the Bone Tree and shove my hands into the familiar dirt. I scoop down and down until I feel the flimsy baggie. It's still safely beneath the tree. "He's right, Jake. We can't ask him to stay around here forever."

Jake sits next to me and pulls Roman down beside him. He's not crying, he doesn't even look sad. He just looks brave. "I'm going to miss you, little brother."

Roman smiles. "Do you want me to leave you with some cheesy goodbye quote you can tattoo on your butts one day?"

I bow my head and litter the ground with tears. "Would it kill ya?"

"Well, I'm already dead so probably not." Roman grabs our hands. "I hope you know I'm not afraid to leave you guys again. I was when I was still alive, but I'm not anymore. Jake, I know you'll be there for Elsie like I was. Els, I know you'll be there for Jake even when he says he doesn't need anyone."

Jake and I mumble different versions of "okay."

"I love you guys." Roman bounces his shoulder off mine.

"Love you too," Jake says.

"Love you back." I lean against Roman and wrap my arm around his waist. Jake does the same, and we stay like that for a long time. Long enough for me to—for once—imagine a life without Roman.

I close my eyes and smush my face into Roman's chest. I smell cinnamon and fabric softener.

Tears pour out of my eyes. They won't stop, no matter how many times I drag my face against Roman's T-shirt.

In my mind, I see every important moment that Roman was supposed to be a part of but never will be. He's already dead, but now he's going to be gone—forever.

Roman taps me under the chin, and I look up at him.

"Even though I'm going, I'm not gone. I know it sounds lame, but I'll always be with you, okay?" He gives me a sweet, sad smile.

I wipe my eyes and nod. I let go of Roman first because I don't think Jake ever would if he had a choice. Jake steps back and wipes his eyes on his sleeve.

I stick my hand in the hole and grab the last token buried underneath the Bone Tree. "Are you ready?"

"Yes." Roman stands up and stretches out his hand toward me. "Let me have it."

I pull out the murky baggie of Roman's blood and hair and pass it to Roman.

Roman doesn't scream or explode—he just flickers with a smile on his face. Passing like a sweet breeze, leaving Jake and me in a mist of fabric softener and cinnamon. I don't know who reaches for each other first, but seconds after Roman disappears, I'm surrounded by Jake's sweatshirt. We cling to each other and cry all the tears we didn't want Roman to see. When I come up for air, I notice something happening to the Bone Tree.

"Jake, look." I wipe my eyes and slide my fingers through Jake's.

Color races up the trunk of the Bone Tree, turning the white bark to a healthy brown. Red leaves sprout from the tips of the branches, and I grin when I realize that the leaves are the exact same color as Roman's hoodie.

Jake squeezes my hand. "See ya, Roman."

I suck in a deep breath, and a smile takes over my face. "Romeo Oxford, this is Echo Lima, over and out."

About The Author

Jenna Lehne is a tea-sipping, horror-loving mom of two boys, and a kitten named Lemons, in Calgary, Alberta. She's a fourth-year Pitch Wars mentor and contributor on the blog MidnightSocietyTales.com. Her short story published in the horror anthology, *Betty Bites Back*. *Bone Tree* is her debut middle-grade novel.

CPSIA information can be obtained
at www.ICGtesting.com
Printed in the USA
LVHW021330270321
682676LV00024B/829/J